Winner Takes All

candy apple books... just for you.

The Accidental Cheerleader by Mimi McCoy

The Boy Next Door by Laura Dower

Miss Popularity by Francesco Sedita

How to Be a Girly Girl in Just Ten Days by Lisa Papademetriou

Drama Queen by Lara Bergen

The Babysitting Wars by Mimi McCoy

Totally Crushed by Eliza Willard

I've Got a Secret by Lara Bergen

Callie for President by Robin Wasserman

Making Waves by Randi Reisfeld and H. B. Gilmour

The Sister Switch by Jane B. Mason and Sarah Hines Stephens

Accidentally Fabulous by Lisa Papademetriou

Confessions of a Bitter Secret Santa by Lara Bergen

Accidentally Famous by Lisa Papademetriou

Star-Crossed by Mimi McCoy

Accidentally Fooled by Lisa Papademetriou

Miss Popularity Goes Camping by Francesco Sedita

Life, Starring Me! by Robin Wasserman

Juicy Gossip by Erin Downing

Accidentally Friends by Lisa Papademetriou

Snowfall Surprise by Jane B. Mason and Sarah Hines Stephens

The Sweetheart Deal by Holly Kowitt

Super Sweet 13 by Helen Perelman

Wish You Were Here, Liza by Robin Wasserman

See You Soon, Samantha by Lara Bergen

Miss You, Mina by Denene Millner

Winner Takes All

by Jenny Santana

SCHOLASTIC INC.

New York   Toronto   London   Auckland
Sydney   Mexico City   New Delhi   Hong Kong

ISBN 978-0-545-16904-2

12 11 10 9 8 7 6 5 4 3 2 1   10 11 12 13 14 15/0

Printed in the U.S.A.   40
First printing, October 2010

*To student councils everywhere,
and for my mom.*

Chapter One

"No excuses," Celia Martinez said to her best friend, Mariela Cruz, over the phone. "Come over now or I won't tell you about my secret plan." She clicked her phone off and smiled to herself, knowing that her dramatics always worked on Mari, and that Mari wouldn't risk missing out on a juicy secret just two weeks into seventh grade.

Mari was also Celia's neighbor, in addition to her friend — she lived only five houses down the block. It was Sunday and they'd both finished their homework, so Celia knew Mari had no reason not to come over. Minutes after they hung up, Celia heard a knock on her front door, and seconds after that she heard Mari's footsteps in the hallway.

"This better be good," Mari said as she huffed across Celia's bedroom. "The people next door to you have their dog out in the yard again, and I had to run past their fence just to keep from getting eaten."

"Mari, Poochie is a *Chihuahua*," Celia said. "He couldn't eat you even if he tried!"

Mari flopped down on Celia's bed and said, "Whatever, that dog is evil. I know he has it in for me." She nuzzled against Celia's multicolored throw pillows and tried to catch her breath, her long stick-straight black hair fanning out like a dark spill on Celia's bedspread. Celia loved Mari's hair and wished hers were that straight. Her own hair was brown and very, very curly, the tight ringlets springing up all around her head. It was hard to control, especially in the high humidity of Miami, and it always looked a little wild, sort of like a mad scientist's, helped only by lots of gel, sturdy butterfly clips, and heavy-duty hair ties.

"Maybe you need to take a hint from the Dog Whisperer and remember that *you* are the pack leader." They both laughed, remembering the one afternoon that summer they'd wasted watching a *Dog Whisperer* marathon on TV. Neither of them even *had* a dog.

Celia and Mari had met the year before in sixth

grade, when Celia joined the drama club in an effort to revamp her image. She'd hoped to fall in with the cool drama clique at Coral Grove Middle School, but her big win in last year's science fair — a total accident and surprise, as sixth graders almost never won best project overall — had placed her solidly in the school's nerd scene. Celia thought it wasn't the worst place to be. The teachers liked her, and all sorts of students — jocks, rockers, cool kids, wannabes, people from every grade — had congratulated her on the science fair win when they saw her at lunch and in the halls. And at least her crazy hair finally seemed to fit in somewhere.

Her attempts to change her image by joining the drama club definitely hadn't worked. In fact, she was pretty bad onstage — her everyday dramatics just didn't translate to the official Drama World. During her first-ever audition, she'd started over twice, flubbed most of her lines, and her hands had shaken so badly she could only keep them still by shoving them into her jeans' back pockets. The club's advisor even stopped her mid-monologue, yelling "Cut!" like a movie director. "I've seen enough, thank you," the advisor said as she rubbed her temples. She asked Celia to leave the stage and not bother with the musical portion of the audition (which was a relief to Celia — she *knew* she couldn't sing, especially not an audition piece from *High School Musical 3*, which she still hadn't even seen yet). She stayed in the drama club to vote on which plays and musicals the school should do and to help with set design, but she was never actually in the plays, unlike Mariela, who usually got a big part. Still, Celia had fun running lines with the good actors and she had a new best friend, Mariela, to cheer on from the box office.

"So I need your help," Celia said. She plopped down on the bed next to Mari. "I was actually hoping I wouldn't have to ask you, but it looks like I have no other choice."

Mari stopped picking at the bright orange polish on her nails and tilted her head at Celia.

"What could have possibly gone wrong already? We're only two weeks into school," she said. "In most ways, it's exactly like last year."

"That's the problem," Celia said, standing up again. She started pacing around the plush purple rug in the middle of her tile floor. "I was really hoping I'd be able to shake off this nerd image in time to run for seventh grade representative, but it just doesn't seem like anyone's forgotten about it."

"Celia, you worry too much about what people think." Mari sat up and clutched a feather-covered pillow to her chest. "And you should totally run! You'd make a great representative. You'd work well with that girl the eighth graders just elected last week."

"Yeah, Krystal ran a great campaign. Even people *not* in eighth grade knew who she was and what she stood for. And I bet it didn't hurt that she's captain of the dance team and super-popular."

Mari shrugged her shoulders and said, "That's true. I don't even remember some of the people running against her. But even as great a race as the eighth grade just had, I bet you could out-campaign them all."

Celia thought so, too. In fact, she'd spent the whole summer planning her campaign, designing posters in her head, and putting herself up against possible candidates in the final big debate. Her mind was filled with ideas for school dances, trips, and seventh grade–only activities. She wanted to institute a seventh grade spirit week that would end with a picnic lunch, and she would sell the administration on it by pitching it as a way to boost attendance. Celia imagined pitching her proposal to the principal: *I can assure you, sir, that students will respond positively to the reward of a spirit week, and the attendance numbers of the seventh grade class at Coral Grove will soar.*

Celia pictured herself no longer a nerd, but a school rep everyone knew and wanted to be involved with — and she couldn't help but get excited. She'd even secretly scribbled "Celia Martinez, Seventh Grade Representative" in her notebook, on the same hidden page where she'd written her crush's name, Lazaro (Laz to his friends), next to hers and surrounded it with hearts.

With so many ideas for making their class the best Coral Grove had ever seen, Celia was more than ready to be a great seventh grade representative. There was only one hitch: Celia was not going to run.

"You know how bad our school is about cliques, Mari. Just look at Yvette and her little band of dance followers."

Yvette and her friends were the very definition of "clique." They always hung out together, sat next to one another at lunch, and participated in all the same clubs, namely the dance team. Saying the name "Yvette" brought to mind the picture of not one girl, but a whole team of them, all dressed in the same tight jeans, with the same super-high ponytails and wearing the same lip gloss. Sometimes, at lunch, when all of the dance clique walked in together, Celia couldn't even tell them apart. They weren't mean girls; they were just picky about who they did and didn't say hi to in the hallways for fear of tainting their image as one of the school's cooler groups. They always said hi to Mari, but usually ignored Celia, even if she was standing right next to Mari. At best, they got her name wrong, mumbling "hey, Claudia" as they strolled to their lockers.

"Yeah, it's pretty bad, the clique-iness," Mari admitted. "But don't you think you should still try? I mean, you've obviously been thinking about it."

"Yeah, but a science fair winner has never also won the election — it's the kiss of death! It defies our school's logic to elect a nerd." Celia stopped pacing and sat down in the middle of the rug, crossing her legs and putting her elbows on her knees. She tried to look really upset, though she'd thought her plan through so many times, she was sure it would work. Still, she needed Mari to agree to it if it was going to go anywhere, and Mari was more likely to say yes if she felt bad for Celia, so Celia kept pouting.

"Who knows?" Mari said. "There's a first time for everything."

"You sound like my mom," Celia said. It was true — Celia's mom had said the exact same thing when Celia told her she wasn't planning to run for the student council position. "Still, the odds are against me. I'm not running."

They sat quietly for a minute. They heard Celia's mom yell from the garage for Carlos, Celia's big brother, to come help with the laundry — it was Carlos's day to help wash and fold, so Celia was off the hook. Mari rearranged herself on Celia's bed so that she was flat on her stomach, her head propped up in her hands.

Mari finally said, "So if you're not running, then what's this secret plan for the election you were talking about?"

This was the opening Celia was waiting for. She jumped up from the rug and launched into Presentation Mode, which involved great posture, eye contact, and the clear enunciation of every word. She'd gone into Presentation Mode when faced with the judges at last year's science fair. It came naturally to her; she was good at public speaking when she knew her subject matter, when it was her own work she was presenting. It was acting she couldn't manage to do — she could not take someone else's ideas and make them her own, not without a lot of stuttering.

"You agreed with me before that our school is kind of dominated by cliques," Celia said. "And you agreed that certain cliques have certain roles. Am I right?"

"I guess," said Mari, starting to worry. She recognized Presentation Mode when she saw it. It was what helped make Celia a straight-A student, but it was always a little weird to see her fall into it outside of class.

"Let's look at the facts," Celia said. "We know nerds never win popularity contests, and the seventh grade representative election is exactly that — a popularity contest. Remember last year?"

When they were in sixth grade, the winners of all three grade-level rep campaigns — sixth, seventh, and eighth — had been some of the school's most popular, well-liked students. Those winners all ran stellar campaigns and did well in the final debate, but the fact that they were already popular to begin with couldn't have hurt their chances of winning.

"I don't think it's one hundred percent about popularity," Mari said as she absentmindedly braided her hair, "but I see your point. None of the past reps could be labeled as straight-up nerds. In fact, a lot of them were . . . drama types."

"Exactly," Celia said as a smile crept onto her face.

"No, no, no!" Mari cried. She squirmed off the bed and stomped away from Celia toward the bedroom door. "It's a terrible idea!"

Apparently, convincing Mari to run for seventh grade rep — but with Celia's ideas and with Celia doing all the work behind the scenes in secret — was going to be harder than Celia had hoped.

"But you don't even have to *do* anything," Celia said. "It'll be easy. I'll take care of everything. I just need you to be the face of the campaign — just *act* the part. You can totally win this for us!"

Mari turned back to her and said, "But Celia, it's *not* like acting. It's dishonest, isn't it? We'd never get away with it. And plus, I don't *want* to be seventh grade rep. *You* do. So you should just stop being scared and run yourself."

Celia took a step back and her breath caught in her throat. Was Mari right — was Celia just scared to run on her own? Was that what her whole plan was really all about? No, she told her-self. She had thought about it all summer. There was no way she would win a popularity contest, even if she proved to be the best person for the job. Still, the seventh grade class deserved a great representative, and she knew she had the brain to do the job. She wanted to give her ideas a shot, even if she couldn't give the rest of herself one. She had to convince Mari that this plan was the only way.

Celia put her hands on Mari's shoulders and pushed her down so that they were both sitting on the purple rug together. Mari's hair was so long she almost sat on it.

"Look," Celia said. "This is about teamwork, about getting the best person elected. I think this plan has a great chance of working. Do you want all the seventh grade dances to be cool or not? Do you want to get stuck going on lame school trips? Do you want us to have a real voice in how lunch period is run, or how much funding student clubs like drama should get? That's what's at stake here."

Mari looked Celia straight in her brown eyes. Celia could tell Mari was thinking about it. "I don't know," Mari finally said. "If I win, how will we keep this up for a whole year?"

Celia hadn't given this too much thought, but she did know how to answer Mari's question. "I'll sign up to be part of student council as a general member, and then I can just volunteer to 'help' with everything."

"But why can't you just run —"

"It's not that I can't run myself," Celia said, knowing what Mari was about to say. "I mean, maybe I am a little scared. But it's really that I think you plus me equals victory. It's a way of guaranteeing that I — we — win, and that the ideas for making this year awesome get heard. I'm sure this kind of thing happens all the time in real politics. It's all about an image, and I just don't have a great one. You do."

Celia felt a little sad admitting this, but she swallowed it down and remembered everything she'd told herself all summer: *It's not about me; it's about making our seventh grade year the best year ever.* She tried to smile.

Mari pouted and raised her eyebrows. She looked down at the carpet and started pulling at the plush fibers. Celia bit her lip and then leaned in to Mari, putting her hands on her best friend's knees.

"Think of it like this," Celia added. "You're who everyone sees, and I'm who everyone hears. It's like you're the drama, and I'm the science behind it. In some ways, it's the biggest part you've ever played! It'll be like a year-long rehearsal for your graduation performance next year in eighth grade."

Mari stopped pulling at the carpet and sat up a little straighter.

"Well, that sort of makes sense, and when you put it that way . . ." Mari trailed off. After a few seconds, she cleared her throat and said, "The only reason I'd do it is because you're my friend and I want you to be happy, and because your ideas really are great, and it would be super-lame if you didn't win. Plus, it does sound like a really challenging role, and I don't know how big a part I'll get in this fall's play, so I may need the practice . . ."

She looked down at her fingernails again and started chipping away more polish. "I'll do it on one condition: You stick with me at all times. I don't want to look stupid, not knowing an answer to some campaign question. Once I say yes, you can't abandon me."

"Of course!" Celia yelped. She wrapped her arms around her friend and new campaign partner. "I'll never leave your side. I promise. I'll stick to you like Poochie does when you invade his territory," she added.

"Ugh. Just what I needed. More Poochie problems."

They both laughed, neither of them knowing that as far as problems went, Poochie would be their smallest.

Chapter Two

Celia should have been totally mentally prepared for what she was about to do — that is, dance around the truth in front of her favorite school counselor, Ms. Perdomo, as she turned in the nomination form with Mariela's name on it. But there was one thing she was not ready for: slamming into her crush, Lazaro Crespi, right as she walked through the main office door.

"Whoa!" Laz yelled as she stepped on his brand-new Jordans. Her face collided with his shoulder, and she saw the red blur of his Miami Heat jersey as she stumbled backward.

As she regained her balance, she rubbed her cheek and cried, "Owww," while trying to think of something to say. Laz, though, spoke first.

"You okay, Celia?" he said, putting a hand on her shoulder to steady her, then letting it drop back to his side. "Lemme guess — you were too busy thinking about the periodic table to watch where you were going?"

"Yeah, because thinking about science is all I ever do, *Lazaro*."

Celia didn't know why, but every time she managed to talk to Laz, they always ended up picking on each other. She couldn't help being really mean to him; it was the only thing she could do to keep from getting nervous and stuttering. At least Laz took it well. He always laughed off her cut-downs, giving her an honest smile and joking right back at her. Though she hadn't been thinking about the periodic table, she *had* used the scientific method months ago to figure this out: Laz's jokes probably meant he liked her — but only as a friend.

Celia looked at Laz's chain — thick and silver and hanging low outside of his shirt. She'd never seen it before. *Must be new*, she thought. *It's really nice.*

"Whose bike you steal that off of?" she said as she lifted the chain and let it drop back on his shirt with a thump. "Or did your mom just put a bike on layaway and all you got now was the chain?"

"Ha-ha," Laz fake laughed. "Actually, it's an early birthday present from my dad. He sent it to me from Puerto Rico. You like it?"

"When's your birthday?" Celia asked.

"Next month. October nineteenth."

"Why doesn't your *dad* know that?"

Laz sucked his teeth and smiled. "I guess I walked right into that one."

"Ya sure did, buddy!" she said. *Buddy?* Why was she such a dork? And why was she encouraging him to think of her as a friend rather than as the love of his life, which she was sure was the case? She slow-motion punched him in the arm, another dork-move.

Then there was a very awkward, very uncomfortable pause. Celia searched her mind for something — anything — to say, just to keep Laz talking to her. She pulled on the straps of her book bag, remembering the form inside the folder — her whole point for coming down to the school's office. Laz blinked and she stared at his dark eyebrows, by far her favorite part of his face.

"So then you're gonna be thirteen, huh?" she finally said, the best and nicest-sounding thing she could come up with.

"Yup," Laz said, looking over her shoulder and down the hall.

17

Think, she told herself. *Too bad you still look like a fifth grader.* No, that was mean, and it wasn't true either. *Is it hard for you to be an age that you can't count on your fingers?* Also mean, and he might not get it. *Are you gonna have a birthday party or something?* There, that was perfect! Casual and nice, and it was a question! Boys loved when you asked them questions, right? Hadn't she read that in one of Mari's fashion magazines? And if he was having a party, it would give him a chance to invite her —

"I better get back to homeroom," Laz said.

She'd missed her chance. Once again, her nerdy brain was thinking too much, and now Laz was walking away.

"See ya," she yelled when he was a few feet away from her.

He turned around, lifted an eyebrow at her, and waved good-bye.

Celia stepped toward the double doors of the main office, trying to get her mind off Laz and his eyebrows and remember what she was there to do. Then she felt the weight of her book bag on her shoulders and remembered: Mariela and the election. She braced herself for the super-cold air-conditioning that would hit her the second she

walked into the maze of ~~~~~~~~ ~~~~~~~~ ~~~~~~~~
tive brain. She pushed thro~~~~~~~~ ~~~~~~~~

"Well, if it isn't my favorite lit~~~ ~~~~~~~~
Martinez! Please, come in!" Ms. Pe~~~~ ~~~~~~~~
behind her big metal desk. She had ~~~~ ~~~~ ~~~~~~~~
back and parted in a zigzag pattern a~~~ ~~~ ~~~~
her funky glasses — thick dark green fr~~~~~ ~~~at,
though ugly on their own, somehow made ner face
look really pretty.

Ms. Perdomo's office was along the back wall
of the main office. The room was small but bright,
and it always smelled like mangos. She had an
unlit mango candle on her desk and a bowl of
mango-scented potpourri perched on the book-
shelf behind her. Sometimes when Ms. Perdomo
visited a classroom or even just walked by in the
hallway, the mango smell trailed behind her like a
fruity phantom. Whenever Celia and her mom
shopped for groceries, the overflowing bin of mangos in the store's produce section made Celia
think of her favorite counselor.

Ms. Perdomo was the most active administra-
tor. She had been in charge of organizing the
science fair last year when Celia won, she was
the student council advisor, and she'd been the

coordinator ever since she ... Grove's staff. She was the youngest ... the counselors, and Celia's mom once said that that was why Ms. Perdomo was so active, because she hadn't "burned out" yet.

"So are you here to make my day and tell me you're running for seventh grade representative?" Ms. Perdomo said as she rubbed her hands together and swiveled in her desk chair.

Celia swung her book bag off her shoulder and planted it in the visitor's chair. She unzipped it and said, "Um, not exactly."

Once she found the form, which was kept crisp and pristine in a brand-new folder that Celia had labeled *Mariela's Campaign Papers*, she handed it to Ms. Perdomo. The counselor kept the smile on her face, but as she scanned the name on the form, Celia thought she saw it droop just a little bit.

"Oh. Ms. Mariela Cruz! Excellent, excellent." She placed the form on her desk. "Looks like everything's in order, then — for Mariela. You have a minute to sit with me, Celia?"

This was what Celia had been dreading. Because of the science fair, Ms. Perdomo knew Celia pretty well. She knew about Celia's tendency to slip into Presentation Mode and about Celia's failed attempts to join the drama clique. Ms. Perdomo even knew Celia's family. Celia's brother, Carlos, had gone to Coral Grove, and Ms. Perdomo always asked Celia about how he was doing over at Hialeah High.

"Sure," Celia said. She lifted her book bag off the chair and sat in it, hugging the bag to her chest.

Ms. Perdomo leaned forward in her desk and smiled. She said, "I want to know why *you* aren't running."

This was one of the things Celia liked about her counselor. Ms. Perdomo just *said* things; she spoke her mind and was very direct with people. There was no banter, no back-and-forth conversation to warm up to things, as with the other counselors. Celia loved when adults just spoke to her like they'd speak to one another. It reminded her of the way the Dog Whisperer just told people why their dog was so bad: *No, no, no — this is* your *fault.*

Celia started spilling out the list of reasons she'd practiced in her head on the car ride to school that morning. "I have a million reasons, Ms. Perdomo. First of all, I'm too busy with other school activities to run. Second, Mariela is my friend and I wouldn't want to run against a friend.

Third, I wouldn't want my position as representative interfering with my schoolwork. Fourth, politics has always struck me as corrupt —"

"Okay, okay, I get it," Ms. Perdomo said, holding her hands up in surrender. "Once you're in 'Presentation Mode,' there's no stopping you."

Ms. Perdomo crossed her arms over her chest, disturbing a bunch of cool buttons pinned to her blazer. She wore different ones every day. The buttons always said weird, random things, like "Area Woman" or "Fancy Pants." Today's button read BUTTON, and the one underneath it said IRONY. She wore a third one that just had the face of a very old dog on it — one of Celia's longtime favorites.

"So if you're turning in this form for her," Ms. Perdomo said, "does that mean you'll be helping Mariela with her campaign as her 'campaign manager'?"

Ms. Perdomo held her arms out and made air quotes with her fingers around the words "campaign manager." If Celia hadn't been so suddenly worried about what Ms. Perdomo might really be asking, she would have laughed. Ms. Perdomo did air quotes way too much, and it was the only thing that seemed lame and teacher-ish about her.

"It would be safe for you to assume that, yes, but it's not what you think —"

Ms. Perdomo covered her ears with her hands and sang, "La la la, I can't hear you! I can't hear your excuses for why you aren't running! La la la."

Celia stopped talking and tried to smile. Sometimes she thought Ms. Perdomo could use a counselor herself, but that was why she loved her. Ms. Perdomo's hands came down.

"I accept this form, which officially makes Mariela a candidate for seventh grade representative to the student council. There. You happy?"

"Very," Celia said. She almost breathed a sigh of relief. Almost.

"Well, I'm not," Ms. Perdomo said.

Here it comes, Celia thought, glad she hadn't taken that breath. Now Ms. Perdomo was going to admit she was onto Celia's plan and forbid her from following through on it. Here came the long talk about self-confidence, about being true to yourself. Here came Ms. Perdomo's crazy claim that a nerdy girl with a semi-Afro and crooked teeth could actually win a popularity contest. It was all the stuff counselors were supposed to say, but that Celia was sure they couldn't possibly *believe*.

But to Celia's surprise, Ms. Perdomo wasn't onto her plan — she didn't even mention that stuff. She said something much worse.

"I'm not happy," she said, "because including Mariela, there are only two people running for seventh grade rep. And two people isn't going to be any fun, for me, anyway. I barely know this other student — he's not one of my advisees."

Ms. Perdomo sat on her side of the desk and frowned.

"I wish I could help you," Celia said. And she meant it.

"Maybe you can," she answered. "I'm not too familiar with this person. Maybe you are?"

Ms. Perdomo slid the filled-out form of the other candidate across her desk and turned it so that Celia could read it. Celia stood up from the chair to see the name on it. As she read it, she felt her knees get wobbly and her heart thud in her chest. She sensed her eyes widening and checked herself, not wanting Ms. Perdomo to register the shock.

The counselor asked, "I know the seventh grade class is huge, but what do you know about Mariela's only opponent so far, Mr. Lazaro 'Laz' Crespi?"

Chapter Three

"Oh no. Please no," Celia whispered under her breath the next morning as the principal's voice boomed through the loudspeaker. He was wrapping up his daily contribution to the morning announcements, a segment he called the "Principal's Proclamations." Celia sat in homeroom, the shock of the disastrous news still buzzing in her ears: According to that Tuesday's Proclamations, the election for seventh grade student council rep was officially between only two people: Mari and Laz.

"This can't be happening," Celia mumbled as she let her head fall to her desk. The principal's voice droned on. "And so, I expect all seventh graders to follow the example of the recently concluded eighth grade campaign and take this election seriously and vote based on the issues. Know that the sixth graders are watching you and that you need to be a good example for them, as their campaigns will begin in the next weeks. And, Coral Grovers, be sure to ask the candidates questions when they visit your homerooms next week. And of course, dear students, the campaign will conclude with the Representative Debate next Friday, where I expect all in attendance to behave in a *respectful* manner. And students, for those of you who don't know what I mean by that, I define *respectful* as follows —"

It was hard enough to listen to the Principal's Proclamations on a regular day (largely thanks to his habit of reminding himself who he was talking to at the beginning of every sentence), but to hear him spell out the next week and a half of the campaign — a campaign between Celia's best friend (and, in reality, Celia herself) and The Love of Her Life Since Fifth Grade — made her stomach knot in a way that caused her to wonder if she should ask for a bathroom pass. Maybe she would run into an equally upset Mariela on her way there — she was in a different homeroom, and though they had most of their classes together, they wouldn't really get a chance to talk about this latest campaign development until their lunch period. Celia thought about raising her hand to get a pass out of there, but the principal was still talking, going on and on about what would and would not be tolerated at any school function. Celia figured it was a list the principal was fond of reciting, since he mentioned it during the Principal's Proclamations at least once a week.

". . . no talking to your neighbor *for any reason*, no leaving your seat *for any reason*, no throwing of any objects *for any reason* . . ."

Celia once asked her mom during the ride home from school why the principal was so focused on discipline and order, hoping to hear some crazy story: Maybe he had once been in charge of a jail! Maybe he'd been kicked out of the military and was now taking out his revenge on the Coral Grove population! Maybe his own kids had ended up in juvie! But Mami had kept her hands on the steering wheel and answered, "I'd be that tough if I was responsible for fifteen hundred middle school kids. Tougher, probably."

The principal finally finished his Proclamations, and the classroom felt oddly quiet in the seconds after he stopped speaking. But then the hum of other students talking started to rise up around her, crowding her thoughts. Celia had never told

Mari about her crush on Laz. She kept it a secret, even from her best friend, because she knew there was no way a cool guy like Laz would ever go for a certified nerd like her, and she was bound to get over her crush, anyway, so why embarrass herself in front of her also-cool best friend by confessing she liked him? This was the kind of logic that won her first place in the science fair, which was why she planned on sticking with it.

But the fact that Laz was her crush wasn't the only problem. Because he was one of the funniest and best-looking kids in seventh grade, Laz was really cool and had a lot of friends. In fact, Celia couldn't think of anyone who *didn't* know Laz except, apparently, Ms. Perdomo. He had a place in almost every clique: He got small parts in the plays, time on the basketball court, and even an honorable mention in the science fair (not for the project itself, but for the art design of his board). Every boy gave him a head nod when he walked through the hallways. Yvette and the rest of the cooler girls said hi to him every morning before the bell rang for homeroom, and made sure to come over and give him a hug on the way to their lockers. And he was just as sweet to the less-cool girls, hence his joking around with Celia and any other nerd. He never seemed fake or insincere either — he was always so...so...*nice*. To pretty much *everyone*. It was part of what made Celia fall for him, and the main reason why he was going to be so hard to beat in the election.

Celia still thought — no, she *knew* — that Laz's coolness would actually hurt him when it came to doing a good job as seventh grade representative. She knew him well enough to guess that he would be too laid-back to take the job seriously. She also knew that he was really indecisive, and — she had to admit this to herself — not exactly the brightest crayon in the box. She'd counted a few misspelled words when she glanced through the report accompanying his science fair board, and the project itself was not actually an experiment — it was called "Mold!" and was just a collection of different things with mold on them glued on the board in an artistic pattern. But that was Laz's magic: He could make mold look attractive. Even Celia had to agree with the judges awarding him honorable mention for art design.

The reason Celia saw Laz as a threat was not because he'd make a better representative, but because he had a better chance of winning the election. Sitting there in homeroom, Celia finally felt like she'd done the right thing by getting Mari to run as the face of the campaign. Celia knew there was no way she could beat someone like Laz, but because Mari was almost in the same class of popularity as him, Celia thought they still had a solid chance. The hard part now was going to be convincing Mari of that.

As they sat down with their lunch trays at the table assigned to their language arts class, Mari said, "This is terrible! He's one of the most-liked boys at Coral Grove!"

You're telling me, Celia thought. She shoveled the corn kernels piled into one compartment of her lunch tray into her mouth, chewing thoroughly. Their table was near Yvette and her band of loyal cool-clique followers, a group of five girls that, along with Yvette, called themselves the Six-Pack. The Six-Pack all had dance together just before lunch period, and they'd sat closer to the end of their assigned table than usual, so Celia was extra careful to avoid getting corn stuck between her teeth. Not that those girls would notice anything Celia did, anyway; they had barely looked her way when she and Mari had first sat down. A couple of them had smiled at Mari, but that was it.

"And not to freak you out or anything," Mari said while opening her chocolate milk carton, "but

I think I have to back out for a totally unrelated reason."

Celia shot up in her seat and blurted out, way too loudly, "WHAT?!!!" She knocked over her own still-unopened carton of milk.

From out of the corner of her eye, Celia saw Yvette and her crew all snap their heads in her direction. She kept herself from looking over at them, resisting the urge to cover her outburst with some lame joke or excuse, and instead pretended to cough. Once the girls went back to their food and started giggling about something else, Celia swallowed hard, trying not to choke on the pieces of corn moving down her throat. She righted her milk carton and coughed a little more. Then she said, quieter this time, "What are you talking about?"

"Okay, so this morning in drama class, Mrs. Wanza finally announced who from second period got parts in the fall play."

Celia remembered that Mari had been worried about this for days, ever since Mrs. Wanza made each student who wanted a part try out by reading the same years-old audition material, a stupid monologue from *Grease*. But with all the campaign plans floating around in her head, she'd completely forgotten.

"And?" Celia said when Mari paused for dramatic effect. Mari gnawed on her pizza. *Since when does corn go with pizza?* Celia suddenly thought.

"I got it." She ducked down under the table, dug around in her bag, and pulled out a huge, thick script. She patted it lovingly. "I got the main part in the play! And it's, like, a lot of lines. Way more than any part I got last year."

"That's awesome," Celia said. She really was excited for Mari, but she knew what was coming next and had to plan her rebuttal — fast.

Mari thumbed through the script's pages and said, "Which brings me back to my point about quitting . . ."

"Are you kidding me?" Celia said. "This news only proves my point even more — you *gotta* run. You're about to be the most famous girl in the school. Once people find out you're the lead in the play, they'll want to vote for you even more. How could you even *think* about quitting?"

She picked up her own rectangle of pizza and nibbled its edges, waiting for Mari's reaction. She was impressed with herself — with her quick thinking and her ability to come up with an excuse that convinced even herself. She swallowed sauce and cheese and saw Mari do the same.

"But, Celia, how will I have time to memorize my lines, practice at rehearsals, *and* do all the campaign stuff? I have to basically memorize lines for my part as seventh grade rep, too. It's like being in *two* plays, and there's only so much information that can fit in my brain at once!"

Mari grabbed her spork and started digging around frantically at her lunch.

"What did I say when I first asked you to do this, Mari? I told you I'd do all the work, didn't I? So don't worry so much. You'll beat Laz, and I'll make it as easy as possible. And you're so talented, I know you're up for the challenge of playing both these roles at the same time. Think of it as being in TWO hit Broadway plays!"

"Double the fame and fortune . . ." Mari considered Celia's argument. She shrugged, then took a bite of corn and said, "Just remember your promise not to —"

"— not to leave your side. I won't," Celia said. "I promise."

Mari smiled at her. She had a piece of food stuck between her two front teeth. Celia pointed to her own teeth, and Mari knew exactly what she meant. Mari covered her teeth with her tongue and made a sucking noise.

"Besides," Celia added, "you can't quit now, because that would mean that Laz wins automatically. Not exactly the definition of democracy, is it?"

"Why are you so weird?" Mari said with a laugh. The piece of corn was gone. "Also, why are you doing that to your hair?"

"Doing what?" Celia said. Only then did she notice her hand, which was tugging at a curl at the base of her neck. *When did I start doing that?* she thought.

"You started doing that the first time you said Laz's name," Mari said, reading her mind.

Oh no, can Mari read minds?

Celia sat on her hand and started talking too fast, saying, "What? That's odd. I don't know why I would do that. That's really weird. Whatever, let's not talk about — hey, since when does corn go with *pizza*, huh? Am I right?"

Mari sat back from her tray. "Oh no. You *like* him, don't you?"

She can *read minds!*

"Wh-who?" Celia stammered. "Oh, Laz? Oh, no way. Noooooo way. He's not for me. He jokes around too much. And his hair is stupid."

"What? He barely has any hair. He keeps it shaved close."

"Yeah, but in sixth grade it was longer and it looked better. Now he looks stupid." Celia only half believed this, but she was desperate to keep from being found out. "And he's — he's way too dumb. I mean, not *dumb* dumb, but not for me. And he has no opinions about anything — people think that makes him nice, but really, he's just not interesting; he has no ideas. How can you like someone who almost never has any ideas, right?"

Mari sat quietly, thinking about this. "You're right, sort of," she said. "I don't know if I totally agree with you — I think Laz is a nice guy, and really cute — but I can see why you don't really like him too much. He's definitely not like you. You guys are, like, *really* different."

Celia crossed her arms over her chest. Maybe Mari wasn't a mind reader after all.

"Don't get mad," Mari said. "What I'm trying to say is that I can't see him being a good representative. Which is why you . . . I mean, me . . . I mean, I . . . I guess I need to stay in the campaign."

Whew, Celia thought. She uncrossed her arms and said, "Exactly."

"And as my official campaign manager," Mari said, "you should know that Laz and his sidekick, Raul, have been staring us down from their table over there for almost the whole lunch period."

35

Celia started to turn in her seat, but Mari grabbed her wrist and said, "No, don't look! I think Laz might be coming over here."

Celia felt her hands start to sweat and sat on them again. "What should we do?" she asked.

Mari raised an eyebrow at her. "Some manager *you* are. I'm going to my locker to unload this heavy thing before next period." She picked up the script and dropped it with a slap back into her bag. "You finish eating and tell me if he says anything interesting. You can tell him I said hi, if you want." She slung her bag over her shoulder and picked up her tray, whispering "good luck," as she headed for the trash line.

A few seconds later, Laz's voice came from behind her: "Celia! Just the person I wanted to see."

She noticed he said *person* and not *girl* — another piece of scientific evidence proving he saw her as just a friend — and she gave a sigh of relief that she hadn't given away her secret to Mari.

"You didn't see enough of me yesterday morning?" she said. "What are you, a masochist?"

Another awkward pause. He blinked and said, "Good one."

"A masochist is someone who enjoys being miserable," she said.

"I knew that," Laz said. He looked at the half-eaten pizza on her tray. "Like, people who eat cafeteria food are masochists."

She pretended to laugh at his joke.

"Anyway," he said, "I saw you talking to the Dark Side a minute ago."

"No, but I am now," she joked back.

"Oh, so *I'm* the enemy?" He raised his eyebrows at her and she almost fell off the table bench. "Well, this enemy," he said, pointing to his chest, "has to talk to you about something." He poked her in the arm and left his finger there for a second. "Can I meet up with you after school somewhere? Maybe walk you home?"

She tried to keep from freaking out. Laz wanted to *talk*. To *her*. Outside of school. He had touched her arm for *no reason*. He wanted to *walk her home*! All of this was new evidence — evidence that suggested a different hypothesis: Maybe he *did* think of her as a girl he could like. It was, in a word, a miracle.

"Um, sure. That would be neat." She winced. *Neat?* "I mean, great. I mean, cool —"

"I get it, Celia," he laughed. He leaned back and

37

wrinkled his eyebrows at her. "Hey, you don't really think I'm the enemy now, do you?"

"Laz, of course not. You're — you're just the best."

She couldn't believe what she'd just said. Even more unbelievable to her was the fact that he was suddenly blushing. He looked down at his sneakers and started to mumble something about not being all that great. Quickly, she added, "Except, wait. I don't walk home. My mom picks me up at the public library a few blocks away. Walk me there?"

Finally, she'd said something smooth and almost flirty — with no mean undertone.

"Can't wait. Meet you at the front entrance by the palm tree?"

"Which of the hundred palm trees outside might that be?" she said. Well, she'd come *close* to not being mean, which was a start.

Laz laughed it off and said, "Right, um, the really skinny one that's, like, to the right of the main doors." He made a motion with his hands, turning them to the right out of some imaginary door between them.

"Got it. So, see you later?" She shrugged her shoulders, and then, trying to seem casual, rested her elbow on the table. She felt the squish of leftover corn kernels beneath it. She looked at it and gasped.

"Girl, you are so funny." He was laughing as he turned away to leave, but it wasn't a mean laugh. Celia figured she'd laugh along, too, and after a second, the corn on her elbow actually *was* funny. "Catch you later." He walked away toward Raul, who was waiting for him back at their table, and then the two of them left the cafeteria.

He'd called her *girl*. He'd said she was funny, laughed *with* her and not *at* her. Mari said he'd been checking her out all through lunch. And then there was that very un-Laz moment of blushing. Could her initial conclusions have been wrong — could it really be possible for someone like Laz to fall for a girl like her?

Conflicting evidence, she thought to herself as she wiped off her elbow with a napkin. Only further observations would confirm or refute the new hope floating around in her head. And only a few more hours of school stood in the way of her chance to run this new experiment.

Chapter Four

That afternoon, Celia waited outside the school by the designated palm tree, butterflies swirling not in the air, but in her stomach. The fronds of all the other palm trees waved at her in the breeze. She'd tried leaning on the tree's trunk to look cool and relaxed, but the thing was so thin that she felt it give a little under her weight, and the mental image of the tree snapping or falling down completely made her stand up straight again. She plopped her book bag down on the grass and waited.

She'd managed to push the meeting with Laz out of her head by fourth-period math, a class she had with Mari. Mari had passed her a note saying only *Anything interesting happen?* and Celia had passed one back that read *With Laz? You wish.* Her nervousness had ended with that, but now, standing outside alone and next to a very unreliable and not very noticeable palm tree, she felt it creeping back into her bones.

She focused on breathing through her nose, having read somewhere that the filtration work done by nose hairs had a calming effect on humans. She breathed slowly and deeply, but it didn't seem to be helping very much.

Other students filed out from the big doors, some of them rushing to make it to the line of buses waiting to take them home. A few people waved at her, then looked confused, as if trying to figure out why she wasn't dying to get away from the building that had held them captive all day. Horns honked from the street — parents signaling their kids to run out to the car so they could avoid the mess of the parking lot. That was the reason her mom picked her up at the library down the street: Her mom could stay at work a little longer while avoiding the craziness of dismissal, and Celia got to unwind for half an hour or so at her favorite place in the neighborhood — inside the cool, calm, book-lined walls of the library. Thinking of the library seemed to calm her down more than breathing through her nose did, so she focused on that — on the library's tall front desk, on the sounds of pages turning, on her lucky worktable near the entrance where she'd come up with the topic for last year's science project.

"I see you found my tree," she heard a voice say from behind her. It was Laz. He pushed against the trunk with both hands and they watched it sway. "Pretty crazy, huh? It survives all the hurricanes 'cause it's so flexible."

She hadn't thought of it that way, and she said so. He gave her a toothy smile and said, "Let's start walking and see what else you haven't thought about."

She felt her face get hot. He tucked his thumbs under the shoulder straps of his backpack and turned on his heel, and she was relieved that his move made him miss the sight of her reddening cheeks.

Laz didn't offer to carry her bag as they walked, which was okay with her; *it's not like we live in the 1950s*, she thought. Plus, that would be so obvious on his part — if he liked her, he would be subtle about it. As they walked away from the school, she listened to their shuffling steps and watched his sneakers glide over the sidewalk.

They fell in step as they reached the cross-walk of the main intersection. She wondered what other people thought when they saw them: *There goes Laz and that dork Celia?* Or maybe, *Celia and Laz are* together*? How did* that *happen?* She wondered if anyone watching them might think: *Look at Laz and Celia — they make a cute couple, don't you think?* Was it really such a crazy, impossible thing? Then Mari's words floated into Celia's head: *You worry too much about what people think.* She looked up from the ground and started walking a little faster, but Laz managed to keep up.

They passed the 7-Eleven where people bought candy and chips in the mornings before school began, where the kids who skipped school altogether sometimes hung out.

"Want anything from the store?" Laz asked her. "My brother tells me that place has the best Slurpee machine in the city."

"Your brother is some kind of Slurpee machine tester?" Celia teased.

Laz grinned and said, "You know, you're one of the smartest girls in our school. And you're really cool, too."

She shot him a look and before she could think about what she should say, she let her default reaction come out: "Okay, Laz, what are you really up to?"

He started to laugh and said, "See, you *are* smart."

Celia felt her feelings of hope deflate a little. She'd meant it as a joke. She hadn't really thought he was complimenting her just because he was about to ask her for some kind of favor. She could see the library building a few blocks away and suddenly she wanted their walk to be over.

"To be honest," Laz said, "me and Raul were surprised you didn't decide to run for representative yourself."

Celia sucked in her breath and held it, careful to keep her eyes on the library ahead and not look at Laz — what if he could see through her somehow and figure out her plan? Had she underestimated his powers of perception?

"But since you're *not* running," he said, "I figured I could really use your help. Maybe you could be my campaign manager?"

She started breathing again, relieved that Laz was just Laz. But then it hit her: Yes, clearly Laz saw her only as a friend. *Oh no*, she thought. She felt stupid for letting herself think that he could have seen her as anything else.

But working with him on his campaign would

give them the chance to get closer, and maybe he'd get to know her and start to like her as *more* than just a friend once he saw how many awesome ideas she had and how smart and funny and useful she could be. She imagined the two of them in her living room working on campaign posters, him complimenting her perfect handwriting, her mom inviting him to stay for a dinner of arroz con pollo. *My favorite*, he'd say; then when her mom left the room, he'd wink at her as he passed her a marker.

It would have been the perfect opportunity for her to go from *girl friend* to *girlfriend*. But she was going to have to say no — and come up with some excuse that sounded realistic, too.

"Celia? Earth to Celia? Hello? What do you think? Are you in or what?"

His voice sounded far away, but suddenly, she was back on the sidewalk, the library right across the street. The reality of what she was about to say crashed down around her. She looked at Laz and saw his eyebrows wrinkle.

"You're not gonna say no, are you?"

"I can't help you, Laz. I'm really sorry."

"What?! Why not?" He sounded genuinely hurt. Celia thought then that if she hadn't spent all of lunch convincing Mari to stay in the race, she might have been tempted to back out herself now. But she couldn't do that, not after the promise she'd made to Mari.

Laz wrinkled his eyebrows even more and said, "You're not helping Mariela, are you?"

Her heart started to beat harder. What if he figured out the plan *now*? Her saying no to helping him had definitely raised his suspicions — she knew how to read his eyebrows. She had to say no to Laz without giving away just how much "help" Mari would be getting from her. She needed to somehow distract him from this fact to keep him from asking too many questions.

"Laz, I would love — and I mean *love* — to help you. But I can't because I promised to help Mari a little with *her* campaign."

"Oh, come on," Laz said, softly slugging her shoulder. "You can stop helping her and just work with me from now on. Don't you think I have a good shot at winning?"

"Actually, I do," she said, and it was the truth. "I think you have a great shot." *That's part of my problem*, she thought to herself.

"Then what's the deal? Why can't you quit Mari's campaign and help me out? Me and you together, we're a slam dunk!" he said.

She tried to ignore the words *me and you* to keep from hyperventilating. Laz's logic was right. She had to think of a better excuse, and fast.

"I can't help you because . . . because I think Mariela might like you, and I don't want her to get mad at me or think I'm going behind her back." *What in the name of science am I saying?* she thought. "If I start spending a lot of time with you, she might get jealous."

Am I crazy? I must be crazy.

"Mariela likes me? Really?" Laz said in a surprised voice. A seagull squawked overhead and the sound was followed by at least another dozen seagulls squawking back. "Huh," Laz said after a second.

This was getting out of hand really fast, and their walk was almost over. Celia stopped on the corner in front of the library and turned to face him, slipping slightly into Presentation Mode.

"I said she *might* like you. A big *Might*. I don't know for sure. You know how those drama kids can be — hard to read."

A tricked-out neon green Buick blasting a Spanish remix through its speakers rolled by them on the street. It stopped at the red light. The driver, a guy who seemed only barely old enough to have a license, looked through the window at the two of them standing on the corner for a second before facing the road again. He turned the volume up on his radio and his car started to rattle even more than before. Celia couldn't wait to be inside the library, away from Laz and the Buick, smothered by the soothing silence.

Once the light turned green and the Buick rolled away, Laz said, "Mari's cute, but I don't really know her that well."

"Seriously, do you *not* understand what *might* means? I'm only speculating about Mari having a crush on you."

"Well, I'm just sayin' she's cute. I mean, I've noticed her around school and in the plays and —"

Celia couldn't bear to hear anymore. She stomped away toward the library doors. He chased after her, saying, "Hey, what are you so mad about? *I'm* the one getting rejected here!"

Celia spun back around. "I'm sorry I said anything about Mari. Please forget it, okay?"

Laz nodded. They stood there listening to the passing traffic. Radios buzzed and engines growled.

"And I really am sorry I can't be your campaign manager, Laz. You have no idea how sorry."

"No, I get it. Mari's your girl, I know." He gave her a weak smile. He looked back over his shoulder toward the school. "I'm gonna go back and get my bike and then head home. You gonna wait for your mom?"

Celia shrugged. "Yeah, she'll be here soon."

"Cool." He took a couple steps away from her and then said, "Are you talking to Mari later?" he asked.

She felt her heart sink.

"Maybe," she said. "Probably."

"Tell her I said hi, okay?"

"Will do," she said. *Will not*, she thought.

Laz looked down at his sneakers and dug into the gravel with his toe.

"And tell her I'm sorry," he added.

Celia shifted the heavy weight of her bag to her other shoulder and said, "Sorry for what?"

"For how I'm going to have to beat her in the election. It's going to be hard for her, losing by so many votes to a guy she has a crush on. Sorry, *might* have a crush on."

"I asked you to please forget I said that!" Celia said.

Laz slid his thumbs back under the straps of his book bag and bent over laughing. He turned and started jogging away, waving over his shoulder to her and yelling, "Celia, you're a trip!" as she stood in front of the library's double glass doors. When he was back across the street, she heard him start to whistle some song she didn't recognize.

She opened the library doors and was greeted by silence and the musty smell of much-loved books. Her lucky table, the place she always did her best work, was open. *Laz really thinks he's gonna win, huh?* she thought. *We'll see about that.* She marched to the table, pulling a pen from the front pocket of her book bag, a storm of ideas already brewing in her head.

Chapter Five

"You have the most perfect handwriting, Celia," Mari said.

Although the compliment wasn't coming from Laz, as she'd daydreamed on their walk to the library two afternoons ago, it was still good to hear. Celia had kept the events of that afternoon a secret from Mari. She didn't need to make her extra worried about the campaign and Laz's plans, and she definitely didn't want to explain how she'd thrown Laz off the scent of the truth — by implying that Mari, and not Celia herself, had a crush on him.

It was Thursday afternoon, still early in the campaign, and both girls were sprawled out on Celia's living room floor, working on a big batch of campaign posters. Surrounded by stacks of poster board, buckets of crayons and markers, and piles of regular-size paper, the two girls were getting a jump on Mari's ads. Celia had heard a rumor that Laz was going to be using Raul's computer over the weekend to make posters (Raul seemed to have been helping Laz a lot since she'd turned him down), so her plan was to get Mari's posters up before the week was out. Therefore they'd get a few days of uncontested advertisement. Plus, candidates were not allowed to cover each other's ads with posters of their own, which meant that the more posters they put up, the bigger the claim they could stake on the real estate of the school's walls.

Mari was finishing up coloring in the *M* of her name with a neon yellow highlighter — to make the name "pop," Celia had said when she'd suggested using it.

"This looks good!" Mari said, standing up and stepping back from the poster to get a better look at it.

"The neon yellow looks okay, I guess," Celia said. She glanced toward the kitchen and whispered, "Would have looked better with the gold glitter, though."

Celia had used her status as a favorite among the school's teachers to finagle the art instructor into loaning her a big canister of gold glitter from the supply closet. After a persuasive speech about the role of art in politics and a small digression into the use of glitter throughout mankind's history, she promised him she wouldn't use it all — just enough to add a "wow" factor. The instructor had handed it over to her at the end of the school day, saying, "Good luck and Godspeed, you little glitter goddess."

But when Celia's mom rolled up to the library and saw how the tiny flecks of gold had already managed to escape the canister and migrate to Celia's hands and face (and book bag and jeans and shirt and sneakers and hair), she said to her daughter, "Don't even think you're using that stuff in my house so that I get to vacuum up glitter for the rest of my life. And put on your seat belt." Celia then tried to use the same speech on her mom, but from behind the wheel her mom had held up her palm and said, "No, I will not be convinced. No glitter. *Punto y ya.*" And Celia knew that meant the matter was not open for debate.

Mari shrugged and whispered back to Celia, "It's okay, we'll deal. Besides, glitter *is* crazy hard to get rid of." She looked at her palms, then held them up for Celia, who saw a couple of specks glinting back despite the fact that Mari hadn't even handled the glitter canister.

"I can't believe Laz is making his posters on a computer," Celia said after a few seconds. She felt herself pushing the marker a little too hard and eased up before she accidentally poked a hole through the paper.

"What, like you wouldn't do these on a computer if we could?"

Mari's family owned a computer, but no printer — her oldest sister had just started college and her parents had given her their printer and were saving for a new one. Celia used the computers in the library, but printing that many pages was out of the question, no matter how much the librarians liked her. She and her brother, Carlos, had already banded together to ask for a computer for Christmas, and since their dad's roofing business was going well so far, it was looking like that would happen. When she thought about how slick and professional Laz's posters would look compared to her own, Celia couldn't help wishing it were December already.

"We don't need technology. People will appreciate the effort that went into these posters. They

54

will know that you care and see you in every poster. It means a lot more to do these by hand than to just click 'Print 100 copies' or whatever."

"We have to make a hundred of these?" Mari whined. She looked around at the dozen or so they'd already done and made a face like she wanted to cry. "I gotta go home soon!"

"For what? I thought your mom said you could eat here tonight."

"She did, but I gotta get home and memorize my lines for the play. We're supposed to have it all in our heads by Monday, and there's no way that's going to happen at the rate I'm going." She started looking around for her bag, peeking underneath a big MARI 4 REP! sign.

"But you have the whole weekend," Celia said, capping a blue marker.

"Yeah, that's what I thought, too, but we ran the first few scenes today and a couple of people are already barely needing to read from the script. Plus my understudy, Sami, was bragging to Mrs. Wanza that she already has all the lines memorized — all *my* lines, that is." She crossed her arms and cocked her head. "How did she manage to do that in, what, two, almost three days? I'm telling you, that Sami girl is making moves to steal my part. She's got Mrs. Wanza worrying that all this campaign stuff is going to affect my concentration."

"But you know that's not gonna happen. Stop freaking out." Celia stood up to meet Mari and put her hands on Mari's shoulders, excitement glinting in her eyes. "Besides, I've got to talk to you about my most recent campaign idea: labels."

"Labels? Like, tags on clothes?"

They both sat back down among the poster paraphernalia.

"Sort of, but I meant more like the labels you put on file folders or envelopes."

"I'm not following," Mari said, pulling a wayward marker out from under her leg.

"We take blank labels, decorate them, and turn them into stickers, basically," Celia said. "I saw a sticker kit at a paper supply store, but using labels would be cheaper, and we can keep whole sheets of them in our notebooks to give out whenever. And when we hand them to people, we can say, 'Stick with Mari Cruz' or 'I'm stuck on Mari.'"

"So now we gotta make sticker labels? In addition to making a hundred posters? Are you serious?"

Celia barely heard her. "I was also thinking," she continued, "about the homeroom visits next week, and that we should really have some kind of presentation board outlining our ideas that I can carry around. People tend to listen more when they have a visual to focus on. And the board will be an excuse to have me go around to homerooms with you."

"Oh boy." Mari rolled her eyes.

"And if not a presentation board, then maybe some pamphlets, or maybe some flyers — oh! — or maybe just quarter cards to save paper, and then we can market you as the eco-friendly candidate." Celia scrambled around for a blank piece of paper so that she could scribble all her ideas on it before she forgot. Sheets of paper seemed to be dancing in the air as she tossed them over her shoulder in search of an empty one. "Maybe we can plan some kind of skit as an intro to each visit, or maybe we can do some improv theater-type stuff to happen during lunch period —"

"This is getting to be too much. Can't we just keep things simple?" Mari said with a sigh.

"Relax! I'll do most of the designing and make most of this stuff on my own. You just need to know what you're going to say to everyone."

"But I *don't* know what to say!"

Celia found a clean sheet and held it up in front of her. "You will," she said. "I'm writing you a script."

"Okay. That's it," Mari said, standing back up. She dusted off her hands and knees and said, "Two scripts over the same weekend? Who do you think I am, Natalie Portman? You're the one destined for Harvard, not me."

"There's your problem — you're thinking too far ahead. Take it one line at a time. You can *so* do this, Mari. And remind me, who's Natalie Portman again?"

"How do you *not* remember who that is? The actress who played Queen Amidala in the Star Wars movies. *Hello?* Those are only, like, some of the highest-grossing films of all time? And Queen Amidala ended up going to Harvard 'cause she's also some sort of super-genius on top of being a famous actress." Mari flipped her hair over her shoulder and put her hands on her hips.

Celia continued jotting down notes and mumbled to the sheet in front of her, "Harvard is *way* overrated, anyway. I'm not even going to apply there."

Mari sucked her teeth and said, "Look who's thinking too far ahead *now*."

"And *script* is the wrong word," Celia said, looking up into Mari's face. "I'm writing up some *talking points* for you. Let's put it that way."

"Talking points. Fine. Either way, I probably should get going." Mari slung her bag on her back, tucked her long hair behind her ears, and folded her arms across her chest. Her dark eyes darted back and forth from Celia to the front door.

Celia felt a wave of panic rise up from her stomach. Mari was clearly starting to doubt her ability to follow through on the plan in the face of play rehearsals, and Celia felt sick at the thought of Mari abandoning the scheme altogether.

"Look, we have the whole weekend to practice," Celia reminded Mari. "And I'm going to be by your side during the homeroom visits to answer any questions you can't handle on your own."

Mari still looked worried. She slowly inched toward the door, looking to escape.

Celia remembered her walk to the library with Laz and how she'd gotten out of that uncomfortable spot by bringing up Mari out of nowhere. In a flash, she jumped up from the floor and blurted out, "But I haven't even told you the latest gossip about Laz yet!" She held her notes in her hand, ink from the marker smudging her thumb and pointer finger, waiting for Mari's reaction — for a sign she could get Mari to stay.

When she said Laz's name, Celia saw something

change — just for a second — in Mari's face. Something in her eyes, or maybe a slight twitch of her lips. But then it was gone, and Celia wondered if she'd even really seen it in the first place. Then again, Mari *was* a great actress.

"Laz?" Mari said. "What about Laz?"

Celia watched for the something again but it was definitely gone. "Nothing specific," she said. "Just about his campaign so far, what our strategy to undermine him is going to be."

"Why do we have to *undermine* him?" Mari wrinkled her thin eyebrows.

"He's your competition," Celia said. "He's the enemy. We've got to be tough on him and his whole campaign — not play dirty, of course, but we need to be tough, for sure."

Mari shifted her weight and pulled her backpack off her shoulders. She let it drop with a thud back on the floor, and Celia was ready to let out a sigh of relief. But before she could, Mari said, "But he's nice. And you know what? I think he's cool. I've always thought that."

Now it was Celia's turn to feel like running from the room. She gripped her notes even more tightly and worried that her white knuckles would give away her own crush. But as she stood there, with Mari staring her in the eyes, she had a new worry: What if her lie to Laz had somehow come true? What if Mari actually *did* have a crush on Laz? What did that mean to the campaign — and what would that mean to them as friends? Celia felt like she was having an out-of-body experience: In her mind, she saw Mari and Laz holding hands and walking home together, Mari and Laz dancing together at Mari's *quince* party, Mari and Laz throwing their high school graduation caps up in the air together, Mari and Laz going to the same college, getting married, opening up some sort of business together — a restaurant, a car wash, a dog hotel. *Oh my God*, she thought, *I will lose them both*.

Mari's voice brought Celia out of her over-the-top *telenovela* daydream, but snippets of it lingered in her head as she listened to Mari explain away her worries.

"I'm not trying to say anything," Mari said, "So don't start your crazy worrying. All I'm saying is he's nice. And kind of cute. I mean, he's okay. And really, we don't need to destroy the guy to win this."

Mari lowered herself onto the floor again and searched around for the yellow highlighter she'd been using. When she found it, she took off the cap and started coloring in the *A* of her name.

61

After a few squeaks from the marker pushing on paper, she turned to Celia and said, "Come on, we don't have a lot of time before your mom yells that dinner's ready."

Celia sat back down, the carpet underneath her suddenly making her legs itch. She tried to shake the feeling that Mari was starting to like Laz. For a long time, the only sound either of them made was the enthusiastic squeaking of moving markers. For now, it seemed that Mari was still her candidate and that Laz was still her crush; for now, there was nothing too bad to worry about.

Chapter Six

In the early days of their friendship, Celia and Mari had bonded over their shared Saturday habit: sleeping in as late as humanly possible. As kids, they'd never really been into Saturday morning cartoons, preferring instead to spend those bright morning hours curled under their plush comforters, basking in the cool darkness they created, the voices of their siblings melting in with those of the animated entertainment. They'd learned they had this habit in common and had both laughed that their moms reacted in the same way — by waltzing into their rooms at noon and yanking the covers off the bed completely, thereby forcing them to start the day.

But this Saturday was not like that at all, because Celia had declared that they were on a mission. During lunch period on Friday, Laz had surprised them both by announcing that he and his campaign were holding an all-day basketball tournament at the neighborhood courts. He and Raul passed out business cards advertising the tournament. One side read COME MEET YOUR CANDIDATE ON THE COURT and listed the details of the daylong event, and the other side, in bigger letters, said LAZ FOR REP. Celia had gotten her card from Laz himself, and as he slipped the little rectangle into her hands, he'd winked and whispered to her, "Cool idea, right?"

Too cool, she thought, trying to ignore how cute he looked in his oversize T-shirt and jeans. Playing up Laz's sports abilities was a great way to show him off as capable and in control — while also distracting voters from the real issues. How could you really discuss your plans for the seventh grade class when you were busy dribbling a ball across burning-hot asphalt? And why hadn't she thought of business cards first? The cards were professional, impressive, and very easy to give out. In a word, they were brilliant.

"I hope you'll come out tomorrow. See you there?" Laz had said when Celia didn't answer him.

64

She folded the card in her hand and tucked it into her pocket, saying, "Oh yeah, I'll be there."

Which was why they were up so early — early for them, at least — that Saturday morning instead of still under the covers in their beds, waiting for their moms to blast them with sunlight.

"Now, remember, this is a reconnaissance mission," Celia said as they walked down the long block from her house toward the park, where the courts — and Laz — would be waiting.

"A *what*? Is that French?" Mari said. She wore her hair long and loose down her back, a weird choice in Celia's mind, since it was superhot out and a ponytail was definitely the way to go — unless there was someone you wanted to impress. Before walking over with Mari, Celia had stood in front of her mirror and toyed with the idea of letting her full curls hang out. She finally realized that her wild hair would only get in her way and that Laz would only notice her for the wrong reasons, so she pulled her hair back and shellacked the sides of her head with gel to keep her curls under control out on the court.

"You know I don't speak French," Celia quipped. "Not yet, anyway. *Reconnaissance*, you know, recon. Investigating the enemy. We're only going so that we can see how many *other* people show up, and gauge how effective this move actually is for Laz's campaign. That's all."

"You're only saying that 'cause you hate Laz and 'cause you stink at basketball," Mari said. A quiet smile crept across her face, and Celia noticed for the first time that morning that Mari seemed to be wearing extra-shimmery lip gloss. Celia looked down and saw that Mari hadn't reapplied her nail polish — it was still the same chipped orange that always dotted her nails — so she guessed Mari hadn't gone completely crazy.

"I actually plan to play a little," Mari went on, shoving her hands into the back pockets of her board shorts. "Maybe challenge him to a free throw contest." She flipped her long dark tresses over her shoulder.

"With your hair like that? All down and flapping in the wind?" Celia said. "You wouldn't have a chance."

Celia felt Mari's steps stumble a little as she walked next to her. So she *was* trying to impress someone? And Celia had just called her out on it?

"What are you talking about? Stop being so weird. I couldn't find my favorite hair clip this morning. That's all. And stop calling Laz 'the enemy' already. I'm only talking about a little friendly competition."

Celia let the word "friendly" echo in her head for a few seconds before saying anything. Then it came to her: Laz's campaign event could actually make *Mari* look good.

"Wait, you're right — that's a great idea. You *should* play him. It'll show anyone who's there that you're a team player and that you're willing to work with people. And while you distract him on the court, I can talk up the spectators and tell them why they should vote for *you!*"

Mari smiled. "Now, *that's* a plan."

A car drove by in the opposite direction. Celia recognized Mrs. Nuñez at the wheel of her trademark banana yellow Cadillac. The car honked hello to the girls as it passed. Mrs. Nuñez was mom to a set of twins — Ricky and Claudia — who were both in the seventh grade at Coral Grove. Celia realized that Mrs. Nuñez had probably just dropped the twins off at the court.

"Just don't let Laz . . . distract you. On the court, I mean." She knew Mari's role in this new plan had her spending a whole afternoon close to Laz, but it was what had to happen if they were going to use Laz's campaign event to their own advantage.

"I'm distracted enough already," Mari said. "I've been so stressed — this election is all I've been able to think about lately. And it's seriously messing up my performance in the play."

Mari dragged her hand through her hair, then lingered over the ends, tugging on them. "I haven't got a single scene down completely yet." She let out a big yawn. After rubbing her eyes to wake herself up a bit more, Mari said, "And being up this early on a Saturday isn't going to help me get any memorization done later today. I have to get ready for next week."

"That's the spirit," Celia said. "As far as the big debate on Friday goes, I think we can have you totally prepped and ready to roll by Thursday night for sure."

Mari stopped dead in her tracks, her feet suddenly cemented to the gum-stained sidewalk. "The debate? It's on Friday? As in *this* coming Friday?" She grabbed at her stomach and said, "Oh, Celia, no."

Celia had to take six or seven steps backward to return to Mari's side. "Of course it's on Friday," she said. "Friday morning, right before everybody votes. Don't you remember from last year? The debate's the last big thing before the voting. It'll make or break us."

Mari stuck her thumbnail in between her top and bottom teeth and began to chew. From across the street and a little ways down the next block came the laughs and shouts of kids — way too many kids — from the park's basketball courts. Between the trunks of the palm trees surrounding the park and the courts, Celia thought she saw a lot of people her own age.

"This is bad," Mari said. She hadn't taken a single step forward.

"I know, it sounds like there are a lot of people there already."

"No, I mean about the debate on Friday." Mari put her hands in her hair again and started tugging at her roots, her thick hair cascading through her fingers. Mari was usually able to keep herself calm — it was normally Mari convincing Celia to chill — but it was starting to look like she was on the brink of some kind of panic attack.

"Don't freak out," Celia said, placing her hand on Mari's shoulder over the straps of the light purple tank top she wore. "Like I said, I'll totally have you ready. I promised you, didn't I?"

Mari pushed her hand off — a very un-Mari-like move — and said, "No, Celia, you're not getting it. The play — our first official run-through is a week from yesterday, meaning *this Friday*."

Celia swallowed hard, finally getting it. Two big performances on the same day, all those lines, jumping off one kind of stage, only to hop onto another; no wonder Mari was being so not herself. How could Celia put her best friend through all of this? Celia stopped thinking about the election and about her own dreams of winning and said what she was really feeling at that moment: "Okay, first off, I'm really sorry everything is happening at once. I really am."

Something about the sincerity in Celia's voice made Mari come out of panic-attack mode. Her hands unclenched themselves from her hair and fell to her sides. Celia put her hand on Mari's shoulder again, and this time, Mari put her own hand over it and gave Celia a weak smile. They heard squeaks and the repetitive thuds of a basketball bouncing against the ground. They both turned in the direction of the courts.

"Laz or no Laz, I really don't have time for this," Mari said, sounding far away.

Laz. Was it him that Mari was coming for all along? Celia was worried, but kept her hand under Mari's.

"We're already here," Celia said with a shrug.

Mari turned and looked back at the row of

houses they'd just passed. Far off they heard Poochie, Celia's neighbor's Chihuahua, barking his brains out. How such a little dog made that much noise, Celia could never figure out. She sensed Mari's wavering and said, "Man, that dog is almost as annoying as Laz."

Mari let out a nervous giggle and said, "You're so mean. He's not that bad." Celia glanced at her and saw Mari's cheeks turning red.

"Are you blushing?!" Celia asked, shocked.

"No, it's just hot out here. Let's get to the courts already."

Celia bit down on her tongue to keep from betraying her own true feelings about Laz. She'd convinced Mari that she saw Laz as nothing but the competition, but if Mari liked Laz, then she knew she had no chance with him. And their potential falling for each other had been all her own fault! She pulled her hand away from Mari and faced the courts, beginning to walk, then jog, then flat-out run from where Mari stood. When Celia was far enough away that she knew Mari couldn't see the tears welling up in her eyes, she turned back around, a huge smile bravely plastered on her face, and yelled back, "Let's go! Game on!" By the time Mari caught up to her, Celia's eyes were dry and ready to focus on the only thing that mattered to her now: winning the election.

Laz looked even cuter on the court than he did in school — something about the way the asphalt brought out his dark eyes — but Celia told herself she didn't notice. Mari, however, let out a little gasp when they first turned into the courts and saw him there, standing under the hoop with a basketball tucked under his arm. Laz waved at them both, and Mari hustled over, suddenly calm and poised. No wonder she was always getting the big parts in the school plays, Celia thought.

Determined to keep her focus on the game as a campaign tactic (and not as an opportunity to swoon over a boy she was suddenly trying really hard not to like anymore), Celia wandered into the crowd, away from where Mari had just swooped in on Laz and the game. As the basketball thumped against the pavement once again, Celia searched the bleachers for influential seventh graders. She'd been right about the twins being there: Ricky and Claudia sat next to each other, sipping from plastic water bottles and eating plantain chips from a bag perched between them on the bench. But maybe they'd planned on coming to the park before Laz's lunch announcement the day before. They were both sort of considered jocks in school — not at all part of the nerd clique: She only knew them because their mom was a childhood friend of her own mom.

Celia recognized a few other seventh graders: Luz Rojas, a girl from the soccer team was there, also drinking from a water bottle and decked out in full soccer gear. Maybe she was just taking a break from her own game, possibly happening on one of the park's other fields. Mike and Henry, two boys with popularity similar to Laz's, sat on the very top bench, looking like they thought they ruled the crowd. Henry elbowed Mike and Mike elbowed him back. Then Henry shoved Mike away and then Mike shoved Henry back. Celia didn't even bother trying to decipher their cool-guy communication.

Though she didn't know everyone by name, she recognized a lot of faces. There was no Yvette and the Six-Pack, and there was no one from drama there either, which didn't surprise her since they tended to be scared of sports in general. Celia couldn't spot a single nerd — she was almost sad to realize she was the only one there. But she knew an opportunity when she saw one: These were not voters she could normally reach — and Laz's event had put them right in her hands.

As Celia surveyed the crowd, she made a mental note to sit next to each of them at some point that afternoon and talk up Mari.

One face that Celia expected to see was missing: Raul's. Celia scanned the bleachers three times before almost deciding he wasn't there. But then she spotted him back by the weathered gray picnic benches underneath the park's barbecue pavilion, just off to the side of the courts. He was standing guard by two big blue coolers, with a clipboard and pen in his hands. It was time for some real reconnaissance, she decided, so she wandered his way as casually as she could.

"Hey, Raul," she said with too much enthusiasm. "Whatcha doing way over here? Not a basketball fan?"

"I like it fine," he said as he scribbled. "I'm just busy is all."

She slid toward him, trying to catch a peek at the papers on the clipboard, and said, "Busy doing what?"

He pulled the clipboard to his chest and tucked the pen he'd been writing with behind his ear. Celia noticed that he had the same kind of kinky curly hair as she did, but since he kept it shaved short, she hadn't ever realized that they had this in common. His hair was much darker, though — almost black — and his eyes were lighter than hers, a shade of brown so clear and bright that she wanted to call it hazel, maybe even green.

"It's none of your business," he said. "But seeing as you were this close to being Laz's campaign manager, I guess I can tell you."

So Raul knew that Laz had asked her and that she'd said no. *Interesting*, Celia thought. But the fact that Raul was filling her in on what might be a campaign secret meant that he and Laz didn't see her as part of the competition. Perhaps Laz had been more distracted by the news of Mari's hypothetical crush than she thought. Maybe making Laz think Mari liked him (and vice versa) would end up working out, diverting attention away from Celia. So what if it meant the end of her crush? Hadn't her mom told her a million stories about all the crushes she'd had when she was a girl, and how none of them had ever panned out? Celia's mom didn't even like Celia's dad when they met — she'd thought he was stuck-up because he refused to dance with anyone at the party where she first saw him — and hadn't they been happily married for more than a dozen years now? Celia tried to focus on Raul's words, making herself ignore the sinking feeling around her heart.

"I'm just keeping track of who's here, how long they hang out for, how they seem to feel about Laz, and whether or not they take one of these." Raul fished around in one of the coolers and brought up a nearly frozen bottle of water. Over the regular label, there was a sticker that read LAZ IS YOUR REP but the ink was smudged and the label was peeling off. In fact, most of the labels were close to being completely illegible.

Celia must have been making a face without realizing it, because Raul whined, "Oh, come on. It doesn't look *that* bad. Maybe I didn't think it through enough, but at least you get the message."

"Another ten minutes in that water," she said, pointing to the slush in the coolers, "and you won't get any message at all."

Raul glared at the label, which really did look more like LOZ OS YOON ROG, and said, "Who am I kidding? You're right. What a disaster." He slammed the bottle back in the cooler, sloshing the water around so that it lapped over the side and onto the concrete floor of the pavilion. He flung the clipboard onto a picnic table and sat down at its bench, putting his head in his hands. He said to the floor, "You have no idea how much printer ink I wasted making those things."

Celia was surprised she hadn't picked up on this before, but it all made sense to her now. Raul *must* be working as Laz's campaign manager. That was why they were using his printer for the posters, that was why he was taking notes on the basketball stuff, and that was why he was so upset now. The whole event had been his idea, not Laz's.

She sat down next to him on the bench, measuring the right words in her head. Inside, she was glad that the labels were smearing so badly, that his really great idea had been foiled somehow. But that still didn't change the fact that it had been a great idea in the first place. She decided it wouldn't hurt her own campaign to admit that to him.

"It's a small part of the day. Look how much fun people are having. They probably won't even notice the messed-up labels."

"They'll notice," he said, still refusing to look at her. "I debated just using a permanent marker and writing out the labels by hand, but no, I wanted to get fancy and use the computer. I'm so stupid."

Considering the small scale of the problem, he seemed almost *too* upset. Celia didn't know what to say to make him not worry about it — she tended to be hard on herself, too. She looked out at the crowd and noticed that people had just peeled off the labels, tossing them to the ground beneath the bleachers. A lot of the faces around now she didn't recognize; there were people from other grades and other schools hanging out. Maybe the tournament idea wouldn't boost Laz as much as she'd worried it would — especially once she made her rounds and convinced them all, one by one, to vote for Mari. This fact made Celia want to be even nicer to Raul.

"Check out Mari and Laz," she said, trying to distract him from his gloom.

On the court, Laz was trying to block Mari from throwing, and he was definitely succeeding. Both of them were sweaty and red-cheeked. As Mari went to take a shot, Laz smacked the ball out of her hands, then caught it as it bounced away from her, running it back to the net for a slam dunk. Some of the people in the stands clapped; others booed. After his shot, he dribbled the ball over to her and placed it gently in her hands. Their smiles were just a little too big, their grins just a little too sweet to be between two real competitors.

Raul, who'd watched the whole exchange along with Celia, suddenly said, "I think he likes her. I don't know for sure. If he does, it's going to be a serious problem for our campaign."

Our *campaign?* — she had to stop herself from saying it out loud. Then her next thought: *So it's true. They like each other and I have no chance with Laz — not that I ever did — but now it's totally out of the question.*

Raul turned quickly to face her and said, "Don't say anything, okay? It's just a feeling I have. Promise you won't tell Mariela?"

His brown-green eyes were pleading, and she recognized herself in them, a sense of something lost, a crush crushed. Could he like Mari, too? Why was everyone suddenly in love with her best friend? She understood him at that moment, and only because she sympathized with his frustration — the frustration of having your heart squashed — did she say, "Okay. I promise."

"I just thought it was better for you to quit while you were ahead," Celia said to Mari as they walked back home. Mari had wanted to keep playing, but they'd been at the courts for more than an hour and Celia had chatted up every seventh grader there. She'd promised to find each of them on Monday and get them a VOTE FOR MARI sticker and they'd all agreed to wear it. But the bigger reason Celia wanted to get out of there was that she was tired of watching her best friend and her crush flirt with each other via basketball, and she felt even worse about it now that she knew Raul was feeling just as miserable. "Besides, I was getting a weird vibe from Raul," Celia added as they crossed the street.

"Really?" Mari said. "Raul? Weird?" Her cheeks were still red from the game, or maybe from blushing. She seemed way too happy for someone who had so much memorizing to do over the next few days.

Remembering her promise, Celia quickly covered her tracks, saying, "Not weird, it's just he confessed that the day wasn't as big a hit as he thought it would be, and I agreed. Most people thought the basketball thing was both candidates' idea, anyway. So no reason for us to stick around for longer, especially when we have work to do."

"That's too bad about the tournament. It *was* a good idea. Maybe more people will show up later." Mari turned and looked back over her shoulder at the park. "Maybe we should go back."

Celia couldn't believe what she was hearing. On the way there, she'd felt guilty for taking up Mari's time, and now here was Mari, willing to give Laz that time without a fight. But she held it in and just kept walking, refusing to look back as Mari had.

"He's pretty cool," Mari went on. "He even wished me luck on writing the speech for Monday's announcements. I thought that was sweet, no?"

"Really sweet," Celia said, rolling her eyes. *Too bad he didn't wish* me *luck*, she thought, *since it's* me *who's writing the speech*. That was what she'd be spending the afternoon doing, pretending to ask Mari for feedback and suggestions when really she already knew what needed to be said — she just needed the time to figure out how to say it best.

"You know, this basketball thing, it's really made me rethink Laz. I mean, this was a fun event that could bring a lot of people together. Don't you think that's the kind of idea you'd want from a grade rep?"

Was Mari seriously betraying her like this? If Celia could overcome her crush for the sake of something bigger, why couldn't Mari? She was so angry and walking so fast that they were almost back to her house now. Celia could already see Poochie waiting with his bark attack raring to go, and she felt like attacking, too.

"You think Laz is so great?" Celia said. "That wasn't even his idea! It was Raul's. So you should just admit that Laz is a dud. He doesn't have any ideas. He's just a stupid guy."

"Oh, so when someone comes up with ideas for you, you're stupid? Is that what you're saying?" Mari came to a halt right in front of the neighbor's yard. Poochie pounced over to them, shoved his muzzle though the chain-link fence, and started growling and snapping.

"That's what you think of me, too, then?" Mari demanded.

"Well, I mean, it's not like you've been a fountain of great ideas for the campaign so far," Celia said without thinking.

"Like you'd even listen to any of my ideas! You don't listen to anyone!"

"That is *not* true!" Celia protested, now more hurt than angry.

"Oh, really?" Mari said. "If you listened to me, you'd be running for rep yourself instead of forcing me into this messed-up scheme of yours!"

"Forcing you? Remember when you *agreed* to do this? Huh? And you didn't seem to mind Laz wishing you luck on the campaign trail, right? You don't seem to mind taking credit for my ideas around *him*."

Mari stood there with her mouth hanging open. The only sound for miles seemed to be stupid Poochie, announcing their fight to the world with every bark.

"That's what you *wanted* me to do!" Mari yelled.

"Yeah, but my ideas aren't meant to help you flirt with the enemy. Or were you just *acting* like you liked him?"

Poochie stared growling so fiercely now that Celia thought he'd somehow caught rabies in the last twenty minutes.

"So that's how you're gonna be, then?" Mari asked. "You're gonna be all weird and jealous because I'm doing what you *told me to do*? Fine. We'll see how you do without me on Monday, when it's time for me to read *your* stupid speech and I'm not there. We'll see how you explain yourself to Ms. Perdomo then. Or will she even get angry? Since you kiss up to her so much, she'll probably let you off the hook."

Now Celia's mouth was hanging open, but Mari's flair for the dramatic gave her insult a perfect ending: She spun on her heel, her long black hair almost slapping Celia in the face as she turned away, and marched back toward her own house. Poochie followed her as she stomped past the fence, growling with so much might that he trembled. He snapped at her ankles, but unlike every other time Mari had had to cross Poochie's path, Mari was so furious she barely noticed the runty dog trying to scare her off.

Poochie stood at the corner of his yard and barked long after Mari walked away, and when he finally understood that she wasn't coming back, he ran back to where Celia stood and started yapping at her.

"Arf arf arf arf arf arf arf arf arf —"

"SHUT UP!" Celia finally yelled. The dog squeaked and tucked his tail between his legs, scooting away from her as fast as he could. In the quiet that followed, she heard her voice and the last of Poochie's barks echo off the concrete balconies of the apartment building across the street. As the dog ran into his owner's house, the shock of the whole argument started to settle on her. At that moment, Poochie was a genius: Running home seemed like the best idea in the whole world.

Chapter Seven

"I really think it's meningitis, Mami," Celia said from under the covers Monday morning when her mom came to drag her out of bed. "I've never been so sure of anything in my life." She let out a little cough, but her mother pulled the sheets off of her, anyway.

"This is the third time you've had meningitis this year," her mom said. "I wanna know what's going on. Just tell me what happened with you and Mari already. You know you're going to school no matter what."

Celia coughed harder and said, "I would tell you, but this meningitis is really —"

"You don't have meningitis. I don't know why I let you watch those PBS specials. The things you pick up!" Celia's mom sat down on the bed. "Now, tell me what happened between you and Mari before I attack you with kisses. I know you want to spill it."

This was true. Celia had spent most of Saturday and all of Sunday almost telling her mom about the fight out on the sidewalk. What had kept her from coming clean was the fact that every time she went through the story in her head, there was no way to make Mari look like the only bad one — and there was no way to get around confessing the truth about who was *really* running for seventh grade rep. She knew she'd eventually come clean about that to her mom, but she wanted to wait, especially now that Mari's whole involvement in the plan might be over.

"Why did you write that speech for Mari?" her mom asked, gesturing with her head over to Celia's desk, which had a cup full of pens and several clean pads of paper on it. On the very top pad, Celia had neatly written out the final version of Mari's speech, which she'd worked on all day Sunday between meals and the half conversations with her mom. The garbage can on the floor under the desk was packed with balled-up yellow sheets — her early attempts at hammering out the right words for Mari to read over the PA system come Monday morning. And now it was that day, and Celia was trying to do everything she could to keep from going to school and facing the prospect of explaining why Mari wasn't there to read the speech herself.

Celia was almost positive Mari was in her own house, trying to get out of going to school, too, but she was the better actress and therefore usually more successful at getting out of things. But Celia secretly worried that Mari *would* go to school, head straight for Ms. Perdomo's office, and confess everything. The risk of that happening was enough to make Celia sit up in bed and swing her legs over the edge, ready to stand. Celia had to get there first to keep Mari from selling her out.

"You're cured!" Mami clapped.

"Yeah, sort of," Celia moaned. She scratched her curly head and said, "I wrote the speech to help her. That's all. I didn't really do it *for* her. I was just trying to . . . help."

"To help, huh? Well, that's good. Helping is good. As long as that's all that's going on — just helping."

"Just helping," Celia said. There was no doubt in Celia's mind that her mom was an actual and honest-to-God mind reader. She always knew what was really going on without Celia ever having to say anything. It was part of why they were so close, and just one of many reasons why she loved her mom so much. Still, Celia couldn't come clean just yet, so she told her, "I promise to talk to you about all this soon. Right now, though, we better hurry if I'm going to make it to school early enough to — um — help Mari practice."

"I'm gonna hold you to that," Celia's mom said as she stood up from the bed. "Just remember you can tell me anything, Celia, and I'll always hear you out. You don't need to resort to meningitis."

"I know, Mami. I'm sorry. I'll be ready soon," Celia said. She got up and went to her closet.

"And not that I claim to know what happened between you two girls, but maybe you should wear the red shirt with the glittery stripe down the side that Mari gave you for your birthday last year," Mami said. "Might be a nice thing to do, you know? Let her know you're sorry?"

Just as Celia thought, *You're so right*, she turned to the door and smiled, but her mom had already slipped out from the room, leaving Celia to get dressed and to think about her next move.

"Hooray! You're here!" Ms. Perdomo shouted as Celia entered her office ten minutes before the first homeroom bell rang. The counselor was putting on eyeliner while holding a little mirror in her hand. The eyeliner was purple, but it didn't look too purple once it surrounded Ms. Perdomo's eyes — it only made her large brown eyes pop even more. She kept outlining her lids as Celia entered the mango-scented room, her hand steady on the pencil. Her pins today read READ 'EM & WEEP! and YOWZA.

"You were expecting me?" Celia said, worried that Mari had somehow gotten to Ms. Perdomo first.

Ms. Perdomo snapped the mirror case shut and clicked the eyeliner back into its skinny tube. She shoved both in a desk drawer and then said, "Well, no. I wasn't. Not really. I mean, I know it's your friend Mariela who's running, but I figured — I mean, I was hoping — you'd come along for moral support. You kids and your moral support. Lazaro has his moral support here this morning, so I figured you'd show up with Mari. Except that Mari isn't here yet . . ." Ms. Perdomo bent forward and looked out her door into the main office.

Celia noticed two book bags on the floor and knew instantly who they must belong to — Laz and Raul. So Raul had come along to watch

Laz give his speech? Or maybe he just wanted to get a close glimpse of Mari to start his morning?

"They're practicing in the boys' bathroom. Isn't that cute? I guess they've got some 'surprises' planned." The famous air quotes. Celia guessed by their energetic appearance that Ms. Perdomo was already on her third cup of coffee that morning. "We're just waiting on Mariela, but don't worry. There's plenty of time before the homeroom bell. I guess Mari's feeling more confident in her speech than Laz is in his."

"Yeah, that's probably it," Celia said, swallowing hard.

"Makes you wonder why she needs you for 'moral support,' though, if she's feeling 'confident.' Excuse me, I need a 'warm-up' big-time." Ms. Perdomo grabbed her coffee cup and dashed out of the room, taking her air quotes with her.

Celia tried to think. What was she going to do? Should she make up an excuse for Mari and then hope that she could convince her later to stay in the race? Should she come clean to Ms. Perdomo and risk losing her status as one of the school's most trustworthy students? Should she leave before Ms. Perdomo came back? She couldn't just bail and leave Mari to get in trouble for not showing up; she'd already gotten Mari into enough of a mess, and until they decided otherwise, they were still best friends.

"You're here."

Celia felt her heart jump. She turned to see Mari standing in the doorway. Mari wore the big silver hoop earrings that Celia had given her last Christmas. She almost never wore them to school because they were too nice — Mari's mom didn't let her wear her nicest jewelry to school. Her mom must have made an exception. Celia stood up from the chair and rushed to the door.

"Mari, I'm so sorry I said —"

"Celia, I feel so bad for saying —"

The two girls crashed into a hug, each of them smothering her apology in the other girl's shoulder. They separated quickly, realizing that Ms. Perdomo could be watching — or worse, Laz and Raul.

"I couldn't let you get in trouble," Mari whispered after looking around the office. "We're already in too deep, huh?"

"Probably," Celia said. "But at least we're prepared." She went into her bag and dug out the legal pad with the speech neatly written out in her crisp handwriting. She handed over the pad along with a pencil. In printing the speech, she'd skipped every other line to make it easier for Mari to read on the fly.

"I can't believe you still wrote it," Mari said.

"I couldn't let you get into trouble either. Besides, you needed to spend Sunday working on your lines for the play."

Mari nodded, grateful for a quality speech. She'd decided to be short and brief in whatever she'd say, but even with only six minutes to go now, she still hadn't written anything out.

Celia tapped the pencil and added, "This is for anything you want to add or change. You're the one who has to read it, so you should have a say in it. "

Mari gave Celia her toothiest smile and said, "Thank you so much for that. But you know what? I totally trust you, and I know I can't improve on your masterpiece."

"That's probably true," Celia joked.

The girls laughed together just as Ms. Perdomo charged into the room, a steaming cup of coffee in her hands.

"Mariela! Yes! So we're ready to go. That is, as soon as the bell rings, of course. And where are those two 'cool' guys? They better be getting back here soon, 'cause this show don't stop for no one."

Mari looked at Celia and rolled her eyes, but Celia laughed.

Crazy, Mari mouthed silently. Celia shook her head no, smiling. Mari started to smile back, but suddenly, the smile turned on itself and her cheeks turned bright red. Celia almost asked her what was wrong, but then she heard someone clear his throat behind her and when she turned around, there was Laz, equally red, with Raul behind him, arms crossed against his chest. Celia noticed then that Raul's smile was brighter than Laz's, and more real, and that he seemed to be smiling only at her. Had she accidentally bonded with him over his failure at the basketball tournament? She wasn't sure, but if he was working with Laz, he, too, was the enemy, and she had to think of him as such.

"Good morning, ladies," Raul said from just behind Laz.

"Such manners!" Ms. Perdomo said. "I love it! Let's go warm up the PA system, shall we?"

"Let's shall," Laz said awkwardly. Raul elbowed him hard in the ribs. Celia wanted to laugh but held it in, thinking she was already lucky to have her friend back — and with that friend about to give a speech she'd never read before, Celia saw no need to tempt fate.

After the regular morning announcements, including another exceptionally boring installment of Principal's Proclamations, Ms. Perdomo clicked the buttons on the PA board that meant the speeches were only getting piped into the seventh grade homerooms and took the microphone in her hands.

"My darling seventh graders," she began. "It is with great pride and enormous excitement that I present to you the candidates for YOUR grade-level representative!"

At this point, Ms. Perdomo imitated the sound of a huge crowd cheering by holding the mike close to her mouth and making a noise that sounded to Celia like when you hold a conch shell up to your ear. Celia laughed even though no one else did.

"Calm down, my eager peoples, calm down. Today you'll hear from the candidates themselves. All two of them."

She raised her eyebrows at them and again, Celia laughed. She was a little upset that none of the other three really "got" Ms. Perdomo the way she did. She figured that it was their loss.

"Up first, thanks to alphabetical order — but only by a slim margin — is Mr. Lazaro Crespi."

Ms. Perdomo held the mike out for Laz as he approached the PA system. He held a sheet with his speech typed out on it. As he began reading, Celia saw that his hands shook ever so slightly.

"Yo yo yo, Coral Grove! This is Lazaro — better known as Laz — Crespi coming to you LIVE from the main office. Now, I KNOW you're gonna vote for me for seventh grade rep, but just in case you STILL have doubts, here are some of my biggest supporters to tell you why I'm the MAN!"

At this point, Laz did an impression of Mr. Negreli, the seventh grade science teacher, emphasizing the teacher's nerdier tendencies. There was a whole riff about misplacing his pocket protector that had nothing to do with the election, but it was really funny. Laz then did a surprisingly good impression of the principal, ripping into the Proclamations. Celia could hear the laughter coming from classrooms closest to the main office — even Ms. Perdomo covered her mouth, presumably hiding a smile. But then Laz turned on her, and did a very inaccurate impression of her, mostly just using a high-pitched too-girly voice. Each impression ended by saying they thought Laz was the greatest and they "approved this message," just like in real political advertisements.

"Thank you for your endorsements!" Laz's real voice chimed. "And so, Coral Grove, do like they say and vote for ME. Just remember my slogan: Laz is the MAN! Vote Laz!"

That's his slogan? Celia thought. She looked at Mari and knew she was thinking the same thing. Even better: She looked at Ms. Perdomo and saw the same idea running through her head.

Laz walked back to Raul and the two of them high-fived. Celia couldn't believe how predictable they were — the speech, the lack of any real content, the reliance on jokes instead of an actual campaign platform. They'd played right into her plan — a plan that was about to unfold right in front of them. She held her breath and waited.

Ms. Perdomo said into the mike, "Thank you, Lazaro, for that moderately entertaining and somewhat misguided speech." She winked at him and he smiled, not registering that she was actually making fun of him. Now it was Celia who covered her smile. "Just for the record, everyone," Ms. Perdomo went on, "and not that I need to tell you this, but all those voices were fake. No staff member has endorsed — or will endorse — any candidate. With that said, I'd like to present Ms. Mariela Cruz, your second and final candidate."

Mari cleared her throat and stepped up to the mike. She held the pad with the speech Celia prepared for her in her hands. Her fingers were so still and poised that Celia thought, *Man, she really is talented.*

"My fellow students," she began in a rich, smooth voice, "as you just heard, it's clear that my opponent sees this election as a big joke."

Celia looked over at Laz and Raul just as their jaws dropped. *Just wait*, she thought to herself, her own cheeks feeling warm, *this is only the beginning.*

"That was amazing!" Mari whispered excitedly as the girls hurried out of the main office and headed to first period. "How did you know Laz was going to do impressions? I mean, your speech *killed* him!"

Celia smiled to herself. She didn't know, exactly. It was a risky move on her part, but one she had scientifically calculated. Based on everything she'd seen so far — and on the fact that Laz thought he did the best impressions of the seventh grade teachers and launched into them whenever someone gave him the opening — she thought the move would pay off. And it had. Mari delivered the speech almost flawlessly (she'd stumbled over one word, *emblematic*, but moved past the mistake quickly) and it had made Laz look like an irresponsible goofball who might be "fun to hang out with" but who was "just not ready to take on such a big responsibility."

"I had a hunch he was going to do that," Celia answered. "I mean, what else was he gonna say?"

It wasn't a mean speech. It just pointed out a huge issue: Laz didn't take the position seriously, and did they really want someone representing the whole seventh grade to the school's administration who couldn't take a simple speech seriously? "In a word: no," Mari had read. She then went on to list what she would do if elected. Celia had packed that part of the speech with lots of fresh ideas — instituting an end-of-the-year field trip for the seventh grade class, moving the seventh grade awards assembly to the evening rather than during school so that more parents could attend, building class unity by creating a seventh grade newsletter that both students and teachers could contribute to, and of course, her ideas for spirit week — all of them stated concisely and clearly.

The speech ended with the slogan, "With Mari Cruz, you'll never lose, so vote for Mari Cruz!" Mari had read it louder than the rest of the speech, and it sounded even catchier in her voice. Afterward, Ms. Perdomo complimented Mari on having written such a thoughtful and provocative speech. Celia had swallowed down the urge to say she'd "helped" write it: It was, after all, necessary to the plan that Mari take all the credit, a fact that was only just then fully sinking in.

Mari sang the slogan now in the hallway. "With Mari Cruz, you never lose, so vote for Mari Cruz!"

When Mari opened the door to her first-period class, the entire room erupted in cheers. Celia was stunned at how the noise bounced around in the hallway where she still stood. Luz Rojas, who'd been at Laz's basketball tournament, yelled from her seat, "Oh my GOD, Mari, you SLAMMED him! That was crazy!"

Ricky Nuñez said from his desk at the front of the class, "Are you some kind of psychic?"

As she slid through the door, Mari answered, "No, I just had a hunch he was going to do that. I mean, what else was he gonna say?"

Mari turned back before shutting the classroom door behind her and winked at Celia.

Celia said, "Hey! That's what I —" to the clos- ing door before realizing she couldn't say a thing about who *really* wrote the speech, about who the *real* psychic was. Mari getting all the credit — had Celia not realized that it might be hard for her to deal with that? *I guess now it's my turn to feel like I'm getting slammed*, she thought.

As Celia dragged herself down the hall to her own first-period class, she grumbled out loud to no one, "And this is only the beginning."

Chapter Eight

"Thanks! It was nothing. Just remember that with Mari Cruz, you never lose!" Mari said to yet another person complimenting her on Monday's speech.

Celia leaned against her locker, a big paper shopping bag full of campaign materials hulking between her feet on the hallway floor, waiting for Mari to fend off this latest praise. It seemed to come from every direction in the school's corridors these last two days. The stickers had been a huge hit, and almost every person passing them in the hallways was wearing one — Celia couldn't make them fast enough. It was Wednesday morning now, and Celia had thought the sting of hearing someone else take credit for her work would have worn off. But it hadn't — not by a long shot.

The worst had come from Laz himself. He had stopped at her and Mari's table on his way out from lunch on Monday. Laz had sat down on the empty bench across from where they were planted and said, "Mari, you really called me out this morning. It was pretty amazing." Celia watched as both he and Mari turned red. Celia was shocked that neither of them could hide their nervousness — Laz was supposed to be cool, supersmooth, and Mari was supposed to be a great actress. But there they were, clearly liking each other. Celia thought she might throw up.

"I mean, don't get me wrong," Laz went on, batting his long eyelashes. "I don't like people calling me out on things, but seriously, it was kind of a genius move. I was impressed." Right then, Raul raced over from the garbage cans, where he was busing his lunch tray. He shot a nervous glance at Celia and mumbled, "Hi, Celia. I mean, hey, guys." His face reddened as he hooked Laz by the collar, swooping him away from the two girls. "What are you *doing*?" Celia heard Raul hiss in Laz's ear.

"Oh my God," Mari had said once they were out of earshot. "He liked my speech!"

Your *speech?* Celia thought. She tried to say this with her eyes, but Mari evidently didn't get it, because Mari then said, "He thinks I'm a genius!" A big grin slowly spread across her face.

"He thought the *speech* was genius," Celia corrected. "If you'd been listening to — instead of drooling over — the competition, you'd have realized what he said. And he probably didn't even mean it. It's probably just a campaign tactic on his part, to make him look more gracious than he really is. And what's up with Raul?" But Mari didn't even blink. She was off in Laz Land, leaving Celia alone to stew in her frustration and bus both their trays.

Celia and Mari had spent all of Monday and Tuesday afternoons practicing for the next big campaign event, the last one before Friday's debate: the homeroom visits. Each candidate had to visit all of the seventh grade homerooms over Wednesday and Thursday to pitch themselves and answer questions from students. They would hit the first half of the homerooms that day and the second half the next, alternating with Laz.

Celia was only a little nervous about how Mari's performance in the classrooms would go: Their afternoon drill sessions had gone okay, but Mari had kept her script for the school play open on her lap the whole time, trying to do two things at once.

"I can't let that Sami girl steal my part. Not only was she off book today, but she's actually *good*. Almost as good as me. I'm telling you, she's making moves!" Mari was still way behind the other actors when it came to memorizing her lines — Mrs. Wanza had given her a two-day extension for having her part memorized before "considering other options," as she'd put it — and after their big blowup on the sidewalk, Celia didn't want to say anything about the script on Mari's lap being a distraction from the campaign script they were working on. Besides, Celia reasoned, she'd be there in the homerooms with Mari should anything go wrong. She'd gotten permission from Ms. Perdomo to accompany Mari on the visits to help carry publicity brochures and posters from room to room.

Celia rustled Ms. Perdomo's list of the assigned Wednesday homerooms out of her campaign manager folder. The first stop was Mr. Negreli's, all the way on the other side of the school from their lockers.

Celia checked her watch: five minutes until the bell, which meant only ten minutes until their first official visit was supposed to begin. Ms. Perdomo would make an announcement over the PA system that the visits were beginning, and then they would be off. Celia felt her stomach squirm. She tapped Mari's shoulder to pull her away from the latest speech fan.

"Later, girl. I'll see you in drama class. I really hope you win this election. Good luck today!" the girl said. Celia recognized her — it was Sami, Mari's understudy for the play. Sami turned away gracefully, a long blondish ponytail swirling the air behind her, and rushed off, a cute purple book bag nestled between her thin shoulders.

"Thanks," Mari said to Sami's back. She turned to her locker and mumbled through gnashed teeth to Celia, "Of course she wants me to win. She knows Mrs. Wanza will give her my part if I do. She's trying to destroy me!"

"What?" Celia said, worried. "How does Mrs. Wanza know you can't handle both responsibilities at the same time? Especially when you won't be doing anything as seventh grade rep — that'll be *my* job."

"And how is Mrs. Wanza supposed to know that, huh? As far as she can see, she just has one lead actress who's about to be stretched too thin. That's how she put it, anyway."

Celia hadn't considered this complication. She

thought Mari's status as the star seventh grade actress would be enough to keep Mrs. Wanza on board, but it sounded like they were already pushing their luck. If Mari's credibility as a drama star was damaged, that might hurt her chances in the election, too.

Thinking on her feet, Celia said, "If you can convince Mrs. Wanza to keep you in the part, then once you're seventh grade rep, she'll see that you aren't distracted and that you can totally juggle both things. She doesn't need to know *how* you're doing it, just that you can."

Mari rolled her eyes.

"Duh, Celia, that's what I'm trying to do. But I'm already slipping in her eyes. I can't keep my lines straight. I keep talking about my plans for reorganizing school dances in the middle of my monologue! And Sami is working so hard — she's just looking for her big break; I guess I can't really blame her — but Mrs. Wanza is starting to lose patience with me. She's questioning my commitment." Mari put her face in her hands and pulled down on her skin.

"God! I just want this campaign to be over already."

That makes two of us, Celia thought.

106

The homeroom bell rang, and the students still left in the halls scurried to their classrooms.

"Just try to stay focused," Celia said.

"Focused? Ha!" Mari said as she slammed her locker shut. She seemed like she was starting to crack.

"We've got five minutes to get to Mr. Negreli's class," Celia said. "Just remember everything we practiced, and I'll be right there next to you in case things head south." She put her arm around Mari's shoulders, halfway upset with herself for what she was about to say: "After Monday's speech, everybody already thinks you're the right person for the job. All you gotta do now is seal the deal. Got it?"

Mari let out a big sigh. Celia saw the worry in her friend's face and realized that taking credit for all of this was just as tough for Mari to handle as it was for Celia to let her. Mari wrinkled her forehead even more, looking around the now-empty hallway. Celia said, "I promised you I'd be at your side through everything. Here's another promise: I will not let you lose your part in the play."

The lines on Mari's forehead evaporated a little and she said, "And how are you going to do that?"

"I have no idea," Celia admitted, but at least Mari laughed at her answer. "I have a feeling I'll be able to come up with a real plan, though, once we get these homeroom visits out of the way." She lifted the heavy paper bag full of campaign stuff with one hand and hooked Mari's arm with the other.

"Shall we?" she asked.

Mari squeezed Celia's arm and answered brightly in a fake British accent, "We shall."

"So what kinds of dances would you plan if you were representative?" Harvey Valencia asked from his seat in the third row.

"See, that's the thing," Mari said, confident because Celia had anticipated this kind of question and had drilled it the day before. "It's not up to *me* to decide that; it's up to *you*. My job as representative is to communicate your ideas to the administration in an effective and convincing manner. So I would ask *you* what dances *you* want to plan, and then get a sense for how the rest of the seventh grade feels about that, then fight for those ideas on your behalf. Being a representative is about being selfless; it's about being — it's about being a . . . being a . . . um . . ."

"A vessel?" Celia chimed in from her spot by

the blackboard, where she stood holding a huge VOTE 4 MARI CRUZ! sign. This was their second-to-last homeroom visit for the day, and her arms were starting to feel heavy.

"Right! A vessel for your thoughts and ideas. So I ask you, Harvey, what kind of dances should we have this year?"

Okay, so Mari's lines did make her sound a lot like Celia. But nobody had picked up on that so far. Aside from a few lapses throughout the morning, things had been going smoothly. Celia propped the poster down on the floor and pulled out a marker and a clean poster board from her brown bag. She wrote "Dance Ideas" at the top and stood poised to write.

"Um, I think . . ." Harvey said. People at the back of the room started to giggle, and someone else yelled, "Shut up!"

"I think," Harvey said, "we should do, like, Under the Sea?"

Celia heard a couple more giggles as she printed "Under the Sea/Nautical theme" on the poster board, but Mari acted really, really excited about that idea, which was all part of what they'd practiced. "Excellent," she said. "What are some other ideas people have?"

Other themes were shouted from the class: 60s Night, Beach Bash, A Walk in the Clouds, Around the World in 80 Days, Bulldozers.

"Bulldozers?" Celia said as she read the word she'd just scribbled on the poster board.

The whole class laughed. Luckily, Celia had anticipated this happening, too, and she and Mari had gone over the best way to defuse a brainstorming session that turned into a joke session. Except that Mari wasn't talking; she was stumbling over her lines.

"Not every idea is going to — no, wait. Um . . . Although all ideas are valid, sometimes we'll need to — no, that's not right either." Mari started chewing on her thumbnail. She lowered her head and closed her eyes, trying to remember what she was supposed to say. Celia recognized Mari's panic — she'd seen it happen during a couple of the homeroom visits they'd already completed — and stepped up from the board in full-force Presentation Mode.

"What Mari means to say is, she obviously can't go back to the principal with a thousand different ideas, so part of her job is to see what ideas most people can agree on, and then take those to him. So, yes, although 'Bulldozers' is a really funny idea here in this class, it's probably not going to fly with the administration. That's what you're try-ing to say, right, Mari?"

Just then, Mari's head snapped up and she yelled to the class, "Fat swine! If you dare breathe one balmy zephyr more, I'll fan your cheeks for you!"

The class sat, stunned, none of them recogniz-ing the line from the play.

"That's not it either, is it?" she said to her thumbnail.

"Uh, is she crazy?" Harvey asked seriously.

"No, no, no!" Celia said, laughing too hard. "Mari's in the school play — she's the lead, actually — and she's just giving you guys a sneak preview of her big performance. Wasn't she con-vincing? She'll be just as convincing as your representative, taking your ideas to the top! Ha-ha-ha!"

The class sat uncomfortably for a second. The teacher cleared his throat and said, "Any other questions for these young ladies before they head out?"

Mari snapped out of her line-searching trance, smiling and poised again. Celia rushed over to the bag and pulled out the stack of MARI 4 REP quarter cards she'd made after school the day before, each one outlining Mari's positions and platform.

She handed them to the first person in each row of seats and asked them to pass them back.

The Bulldozers jerk decided to get in one more joke before the ordeal was over. "Hey, Mariela," he said, "if you're the one running for seventh grade rep, then why does Celia seem to know more about your ideas than you do?"

"That's a great question," Mari said, her face turning very white. "Every good candidate has an even better team behind them, and Celia is on my team."

This answer was from the script, but Celia had assured Mari during their run-through that it was solely in case of an emergency, that no one would ask that. As Celia scrambled to get the last of the quarter cards passed out, the teacher said, "Thank you, ladies," as the rest of the class clapped.

Once they were safely outside the classroom, Mari grabbed Celia by the arms and said, "You see? People are figuring it out! I can't keep doing this. I look like a fool!"

"Mari, you're doing great. You handled that last question with a lot of grace."

"Yeah, and two seconds before that I called them fat swine! My head is totally crammed with too many phrases!"

"Keep your voice down. Someone will hear you."

Celia shot a look over Mari's shoulder to indicate who that someone was: Laz, coming down the hall, heading to his last homeroom of the morning. Weirdly, he was also yelling something, but Raul, who walked next to him carrying a big bag of Life Savers candies in a bin that said LAZ IS THE MAN! shushed him before they could hear anything specific.

Laz gave Raul a nasty look and then started to march over to them. Celia heard Mari suck in air and say, "Oh my God," just before standing up even straighter. She turned to Celia and whispered, "Do I look okay?"

Celia couldn't speak. She just nodded. As always, Mari looked beautiful. Celia stood there with her big brown bag, lighter now that she'd given almost everything out, and watched the two of them talk.

"How are your visits going?" Laz said as he put his hands in his jeans pockets. He wore a long-sleeved button-down shirt untucked, but with a tie. It was a cool, laid-back style. The tie was probably an effort to look more serious, something he'd need to do if he was going to refute Mari's campaign's biggest argument against him.

113

"Oh, you know. Great. Really great."

Really great? Celia thought. Did Laz actually think that Mari and her "really greats" could have written that speech from Monday? The real genius was standing right there in plain sight. He hadn't even said hi to her.

Raul stomped over, the wrappers on the Life Savers squeaking against one another. When Celia glanced in the bin, she saw that it was nearly full.

"You haven't been giving those out?" she blurted.

Laz finally looked at her. "No, we couldn't. We started to, but Ms. Perdomo said that giving out candy constituted bribery and she made us stop. By the way, great idea, Raul."

"Oh, *now* it's my idea?"

Celia thought she saw a much bigger fight brewing between them, but they left it at that. There was an awkward silence.

"Hey," Celia finally said, "did it occur to you guys that you could have put 'Laz is a Life Saver' on the bin instead of 'Laz is the Man'? I mean, no offense, but it's almost obvious."

"Celia, come on, that's just mean," Mari said. Celia couldn't believe it.

"That's just how Celia talks," Laz said. "You're not used to her by now?"

The two of them laughed, leaning into each other and being all chummy. Celia stood there, wanting to flip over the bin of Life Savers and bury Mari and Laz in her candy-coated wrath.

"Actually, I *did* think of that," Raul said, stopping the laughs cold. He looked happy to have Celia on his side, even if it was only for a second. "Mr. Super-Fly over here feels that slogans are dorky. But he's wrong."

The smile suddenly gone, Laz turned to Raul with a fierce scowl on his face. Celia caught it and held a laugh in her throat.

"We should get going," Laz said without breaking his stare at Raul.

"You're the one who wanted to come over here and talk to the enemy," Raul said back, shrugging his shoulders. "I'm just your lowly campaign manager."

"Enough already, okay, Raul? Let's get out of here." Laz stomped away toward the last homeroom door for the morning, his neck and face burning red.

"You're the boss," Raul said, lugging the Life Savers bin down the hall. "Later, Mari. Bye, Celia — see you later, maybe?" he called over his shoulder.

"Okay, that was weird," Mari said once the boys were gone from the hallway.

"Thanks for calling me mean. That really makes me feel good about myself," Celia said in a dead-pan voice.

"Oh, please, Celia. I was just standing up for Laz. I feel bad for him, kind of. And besides, doesn't everything I'm doing for this campaign clearly show that my loyalty is to you?"

"I'm not so sure," Celia joked, though she did mean it a little, especially after the way Mari blatantly flirted with Laz, who was, up until very recently, her crush. Though, of course, Mari didn't know that. "Let's see how this last homeroom visit goes and I'll tell you then." Celia smiled, hiding her doubts with a little acting of her own.

Chapter Nine

"Flash cards, check. Stopwatch, check."

Celia paced around her room, making sure that she had everything she needed for the debate rehearsal she'd planned for Mari that afternoon. The real debate would be happening the next morning, and Celia admitted to herself that she was more than just a little worried about how Mari would do. The buzz around school was that Laz's visits had actually cost him some votes. Celia had overheard Yvette and her crew at lunch laughing about how Mr. Negreli, during Laz's visit to his homeroom, had asked him some basic questions about his reasons for running, and Laz had come off looking unprepared and not at all serious. "I mean, just 'cause he's cool doesn't mean he should win," Celia heard Yvette say, and her followers nodded in agreement.

Yvette's opinion was a good sign for Mari's campaign, but still, the last round of Mari's homeroom visits that morning had been worse than Wednesday's. Mari kept forgetting her campaign platform or accidentally reciting lines from the play in almost every class they talked to. Then, at lunch, Mari reported that Mrs. Wanza had just plain yelled at her for making the same kinds of mistakes in rehearsal: During a sword fight scene, Mari had apparently challenged another character to "explore the broad range of fund-raising opportunities available and have potential outside vendors compete for our school's business." Like Mrs. Wanza, Celia had to face the facts: Mari was a mess. It was going to take a long night of drills and practice questions to get her where she needed to be to face Laz.

"Highlighter, check. Bag of M&M's, check."

The only thing missing was Mari.

She looked at the digital clock blinking on her desk. It was 5:24 — Mari was almost half an hour late. The plan had been that the two girls would head home from school, check in with their moms, shower and eat something, then be at Celia's house by five to start the long night of prepping for Friday morning. Just as she was about to pick up the phone and call Mari's house, Celia heard her brother, Carlos, yell from the front door, "Celia! It's Mari! She's here to play or whatever!"

"Shut up, Carlos," she heard Mari say.

A few seconds later, Mari appeared in the doorway, her hair looking stringy and oily, her pretty skin unusually blotchy. There was even a smudge of ink on Mari's left cheek. The worst sign, though, was that Mari was still in her school clothes — a cute T-shirt dress that now, at the end of the day, looked as wrinkled and tired as Mari herself.

Celia sat at her desk and started shuffling a stack of paper, pretending not to notice Mari's frazzled appearance.

"I'm just guessing here, but you didn't shower, did you?" She faced Mari and pinched her own nose shut. "Now I'm gonna have to smell you all through our practice. Thanks a lot."

"Celia, I —"

"I know, I know. I'm being mean again. Sorry." Celia let go of her nose and smiled from her chair, but Mari's face stayed frozen. "I just thought we were gonna be ready to stay late working here if we needed to, but as long as you shower before school tomorrow, we'll be fine. You've got to look fresh and sharp in front of Laz and everyone at school."

Mari still hadn't come into Celia's room. She lingered in the doorway, holding on to the edge of the door frame. At the mention of Laz's name, Mari had looked away from Celia and stared instead at the ceiling. She now looked Celia straight in the eyes. "I need to talk to you," she said.

"What's wrong?" Celia asked, really starting to feel nervous — Mari still hadn't stepped in the room. "Did Poochie harass you on the walk here?"

"I didn't walk. My mom drove me. She's still here, waiting for me. She's talking to your mom outside."

Celia didn't really want to know the answer to her next question, but she had to ask: "Why is your mom waiting for you? Doesn't she know we're gonna be a while?"

Finally, Mari stepped into the room. She walked all the way in and sat down on the round purple rug, right in front of Celia. Celia thought back to the day she'd sat there herself and asked Mari to agree to this whole scheme. They were so close to winning, so close to being done. In the silence of that second, she heard Mari's mom's car engine running in the driveway, and Celia suddenly felt the week come to a screeching halt.

"Remember how you promised yesterday that you wouldn't let me lose my part in the play?"

Celia felt a little better; if this was about the play, then everything was okay. It was the debate she was worried about.

"Of course I remember," Celia answered. "Not that I had any idea how I was gonna do that, but I did promise."

"And you meant it?" Mari said. Her face looked strained. She looked too hurt to be acting — Celia knew this was real.

"Of course," she said. "I know that the play is as important to you as being representative is to me." Celia's voice cracked as she said "me" — she wasn't so sure anymore that if Mari won, she could handle everyone giving Mari credit for her work. She wouldn't *really* be a representative, not in the way she wanted to be. But it was too late to do anything about that. "Mari, just tell me what's going on. If you figured out a plan to keep your part, I want to hear it."

Mari took a deep breath and sat up on her knees. She tucked her hair behind her ears. She closed her eyes and silently nodded to herself after a second. When she opened her eyes again, they were wet with tears.

"I can't go through with the debate tomorrow. I have to spend the rest of this afternoon drilling my lines for the play's run-through. My mom's gonna help me get them down."

Celia tried to sound calm, but she couldn't control the panic rising in her voice. "But you have to do the debate! It's not *optional* for a candidate! If you don't participate, you're —"

"I'm dropping out of the race. It's the only way Mrs. Wanza's gonna let me keep the lead and not let Sami start in my place tomorrow at rehearsal."

Mari closed her eyes again and added, "My mom already called the school and left a message for Mrs. Wanza with my decision."

Celia realized she'd been holding her breath. She tried to breathe but the air wouldn't come. She tried to think calming thoughts, but all she could do was sit like a statue at her desk.

"This was a really hard choice for me," Mari went on. "I know how much being rep means to you — I only said yes to this whole thing for you. But my mom said that if we're really friends, we'd help each other do the right things. And besides, being part of drama is just too important to me."

Every thought and feeling imaginable raced through Celia's head. She was so lost in her own whirlwind that she could barely register what Mari was saying now. Her thoughts poured out of her in a panicked rant, "But we're so close to winning! We've done all this work! We can't just let Laz win. Why didn't you talk to me about this? What am I gonna do? You just admitted how much this means to me — Mari, I *need* you to do this!"

Mari pulled her hair over her shoulder and started tugging at it. She was clearly trying to stay calm in the hopes that it would keep Celia from freaking out more than she already was. "I know you're probably gonna be mad at me for a while," Mari said. "But I have to take that risk and just trust that you'll eventually understand. At least, that's what my mom says."

Mari's mom — who was talking to her own mom outside right now. Celia snapped out of her shocked trance and said the first words that finally found their way out of her mouth. "So then you told your mom *everything*?"

Mari looked past Celia and out the window. "Sort of. I've been feeling bad, keeping it from her. I was dying to talk to her about what's really been going on. We're like you and your mom, you know? You and my mom are my best friends."

Celia suddenly felt like the worst person in the world. She felt so guilty for making Mari keep something this big from her mom. She'd been swallowing down her own guilt about not coming clean to her mom either, especially since her mom seemed to suspect something was going on. But she'd planned on telling her eventually — she'd just had no idea when or how.

"I'm sorry I'm letting you down," Mari said after a long silence. "But you did make a promise, and this is the only way I can see that you can keep that promise. And if you can get past probably hating me right now and really think about it, I know you'll agree."

All Celia could think about, though, was the immediate future. "But it's just one more day, Mari! Please, don't do this."

"It would have been a disaster, anyway. It's not like you can stand behind me at that podium tomorrow and back me up like you did during the homeroom visits," Mari said, getting up from the rug. "And what if I had won? How would we have kept this up for a whole year when we're barely making it work for a week?"

Celia didn't know what to say. She'd pushed this same worry out of her own head days before, focusing instead on just getting elected. She'd told herself, *We'll cross that bridge when we come to it*, something she'd heard Ms. Perdomo say at least a dozen times. But the truth was, she had only a vague idea of how she and Mari would handle things down the road. She knew people would start to suspect things if Mari kept picking her to work on projects. She couldn't promise Mari that things would get any easier after the election.

"Besides," Mari added when Celia didn't answer, "it's already done. The call's been made."

Celia imagined Yvette and her groupies gossiping at the lunch table about this, whispering Mari's name and spreading rumors. They were going to go nuts over this news — Celia had to do something. She jumped up from her chair and flailed her arms. "But don't you care what people are gonna say? Aren't you worried what everyone at school is going to think of you if you drop out?"

"Who cares?!" Mari snapped. "I can't control what other people think. Right now, I only care what *I* think. And I feel like I'm doing the right thing for the first time in a while."

She marched to the door. Just before she left the room completely, she stopped in the doorway and turned back to face Celia. Her face looked strong, but her eyes seemed tired and hurt.

"You're the real candidate, anyway," she said before closing the door behind her and disappearing down the hall.

A few seconds later, Celia heard the front door click shut. Eventually, she heard Mari's mom drive away. She sat back at her desk, trying to think about what to do while waiting for her mom to knock on her door and let herself in — a lecture was inevitable now.

It wasn't until after the sun went down and she was left waiting in the dark that Celia realized her mother wasn't coming. Maybe Mari's mom had told her mom everything and now she was mad, or worse, hurt and disappointed.

It was up to Celia alone to figure out what to do next. She thought about calling Mari and asking — maybe even begging — her to reconsider, but she couldn't bring herself to do it: She *had* promised Mari that she'd help her keep her part. And the only conclusion Celia had come to while thinking things through by herself was that Mari was right — this was the only way to keep that promise. The next day's debate took a backseat to the one Celia was not at all ready for: the debate in her head about what to do come Friday morning.

Chapter Ten

Celia heard her mom's voice despite the layers of sheets and blankets she'd pulled up over her head to block the too-bright Friday morning sun.

"Time to get up. We gotta get you to school early if you're going to have enough time to explain everything to Ms. Perdomo."

Celia shot straight up, suddenly super-awake, her heart pounding. Her frizzy curls danced around her head. Her mom stood at the edge of the bed, her hands on her hips.

"So you *do* know," Celia said, letting her posture go slack.

"Oh, *mamita*, moms always know these things. What I don't get is why you've been keeping it from me. Do you *not* trust me?"

Celia leaned back on her arms, squinting in the light. "It's not that, Mom." She pushed the covers down with her feet and stared at her retro Wonder Woman pajama pants. "I just knew you'd tell me what a bad move it all was, that I should be confident and run myself, all the stuff you're supposed to say."

"If you knew that I was going to tell you that — which, by the way, is all true and I'm very impressed with my theoretical advice — then shouldn't that have been a red flag that maybe this was a bad idea?"

Her mom didn't look or sound angry; she was sincerely asking Celia this question. Celia wrapped her arms around herself and rubbed her shoulders, warming them up to fight the blast of the air conditioner.

"I was just hoping it would all work out somehow."

Her mom sat on the bed, smoothing the sheets with her palms. She had the same dark curly hair as Celia but it had settled a little with age. Celia hoped the same would happen to her own locks as she got older.

"Sometimes I worry you're too smart for your own good, *mi cielo*." She kissed Celia on the forehead. "But let me tell you, you're going to need those brains today to get you out of this mess."

Her mom started to arrange Celia's curls around her face, smoothing them as she had the sheets. "I figured you needed last night to straighten things out for yourself, so I left you alone — and besides, you haven't wanted my advice so far."

Her mom pouted in an exaggerated, teasing way, but Celia still felt a lump of guilt rise in her throat. "But now I want to hear what you're thinking about how to fix this."

Celia shrugged, then let herself fall back to her pillows. When it came to a new plan, she was truly stumped. She'd spent all night looking at her ceiling, or at the minutes blinking away on the clock perched on her desk. She wished everything could be as simple as a science experiment, with its methods and outlined procedures, and systems for recording results. But the problem had actually *started* when she decided to tackle the election the same way she would an experiment. Celia hadn't accounted for so many variables — Laz being the other candidate, his wanting her as his campaign manager, Mari landing the lead in the play, her and Mari's mixed-up feelings over Laz — that the experiment had officially gone haywire almost right away. She couldn't find the right solution to such a complicated problem.

The only thing that made her feel better was something her science teacher had said last year, when she was struggling to interpret the results of the experiment that would go on to win her first place in the fair: *The best solution is usually the simplest one available.* But Celia had drifted off to sleep without coming to any firm conclusions about her next move.

"I guess it has to start with talking to Ms. Perdomo," Celia finally said. "Coming clean, and at some point soon, apologizing to Mari."

"I would say so," her mom said.

Celia looked at the desk where she'd written Mari's speech — the speech that had gone over so well and had gotten so many compliments. Mari might have gotten the credit, but Celia knew it was *her* speech. *The best solution is usually the simplest one available*, a voice echoed in Celia's head. Then she heard Mari's words: *You're the real candidate anyway.*

"Do you think I should ask Ms. Perdomo if I can take Mari's place in the debate and take over as the candidate?" Celia said.

It was simple, but was this solution really "available" — would Ms. Perdomo even allow it?

"Is that what you think you should do?" her mom asked.

"I don't know. Maybe," Celia said. "She might not let me. But I know I'm right about apologizing. That, I *need* to do."

Her mom nodded, and Celia started to feel a little better. As much as she'd worried too much about random people's opinions of her, she realized she *should* care what the important people in her life thought about her. Mari, Ms. Perdomo, her mom, maybe even Laz — she wanted to keep their respect.

"I'm sorry I didn't talk to you about this whole campaign fiasco," Celia finally said.

Her mom was cool enough that she didn't say, *I know, sweetie* or *I forgive you.* What she did say was, "You're going to be more sorry in a minute when you realize how early it is. Now, get up and get dressed and I'll make you some café con leche to jump-start your brain before I take you to school. From then on, you're on your own. But I'll be thinking about you all day."

Her mom stood up from the bed and added, "We have enough time for me to flat-iron your hair a little if you want. Not that I don't love your curls, but if it'll make you feel better about the possibility of going onstage for the debate, I can fire that baby up right now."

Celia tugged on the tight ringlets now framing her face. If Ms. Perdomo somehow allowed her to take Mari's place, having a new take on her old look might be a good campaign move. "Let's do it," she said. "Only because it might get people's attention right before they go to vote."

Her mom nodded and whisked herself away, yelling from down the hall, "But you have to get up right now if we're going to have time. So don't fall back asleep like you always do!"

But Celia was already out of bed, standing in front of her closet and thinking, *Which of these outfits says "seventh grade rep"?*

Once Celia found herself in front of the main office's big double doors, though, it was a totally different story. Her mouth was completely dry, and the café con leche in her stomach was swishing around more than she wanted to think about. The halls were deserted except for a janitor who was way down the main corridor sweeping up near the back wall of lockers while listening to something through headphones. She waited for him to notice her, maybe wave hello as a small sign that everything would be okay, but he never so much as lifted his eyes up from his work.

She'd tried to keep herself from getting nervous during the drive to school, but had felt the panic kick in entirely when her mom put the car in PARK and unlocked the car door for Celia to get out.

"I don't know if I can do this," she'd blurted out to the windshield just as she put her hand on the door latch.

"Celia, I know you can." Her mom squeezed her other hand, then kissed it. "And I'm sorry, but you really don't have a choice here."

Celia liked that her mom was so blunt. It was the same quality she admired in Ms. Perdomo. It made her calm to hear facts laid out so plainly. It was *feelings* she couldn't factor into her equations.

But now that she was alone and faced with the reality of what she had to do, the facts were just as frightening. It didn't matter that her curls were a little looser and that she was wearing her favorite dark jeans and the V-neck button-down top that always got compliments whenever she wore it. She was about to confess a huge lie, and she'd never been in trouble at school before.

She'd briefly considered stalling — *Mari is sick*, or *Mari has cold feet* — but she knew that would only make the problem bigger in the long run. Mari was going to be at school for the play, so her lie would be exposed almost immediately. And there was that phone message to Mrs. Wanza that Celia was sure Ms. Perdomo would eventually hear about. Plus, she knew that if she were ever going to salvage her friendship with Mari, she had to admit that she was totally to blame for this, if only to prove to Mari how much their friendship mattered to her.

Celia dreaded having to explain everything to Ms. Perdomo, who might not let her take Mari's place in the election. Even if she did, Celia wouldn't be surprised if she lost her status as one of Ms. Perdomo's favorite students. Was she ready to give that up?

On a whole other level of worry were Celia's old fears, the ones that had made her not want to run in the first place: How were the other students going to react when they saw dorky Celia instead of the cute drama girl they expected behind the podium at the debate? Even worse, what if her old feelings for Laz somehow got in her way of debating him? She felt sure she didn't like him anymore, but what if things changed once she saw him onstage?

She heard a rustling down the corridor in the direction of the janitor, but when she looked down the hallway, he'd somehow disappeared.

Celia took a deep breath and placed her hands over her face to block out the fluorescent light glowing up above. She repeated Mari's words in her head to keep her thoughts from spiraling out of control: *I can't control what other people think. What matters is what I think.*

She removed her hands from her face and smoothed down the side part her mom had etched in her hair. Her stomach settled a little — enough that she knew she wouldn't be sick at any second. The doors loomed in front of her, the sounds of buzzing printers and ringing phones audible just behind them.

Just as she pushed the doubts from her head for just a little longer, Celia finally pushed through the office doors, her hope in Ms. Perdomo's acceptance of the simplest solution shaky, but her confidence in it as the right thing to do finally feeling firm.

Chapter Eleven

From backstage, the noise of the entire seventh grade shuffling into the auditorium for the debate was deafening. Celia stood behind the right side of the curtain, refusing to look out at the growing crowd. She tried to concentrate on her breathing to stay calm. Her head was still spinning from the events of the last hour.

Her confession to Ms. Perdomo that morning had gotten out of control fast. She started talking about the school's cliques, about her unhappiness at landing herself in the "nerd" category, and about liking and not liking Laz. She explained how upset she'd been when people gave Mari the credit for her ideas — even though that had been her own fault. A voice in Celia's head kept saying, *Too much information*, but who better to spill your guts to than a certified counselor? She talked nonstop for a good ten minutes before Ms. Perdomo raised her hand to stop her.

"I am very proud of you for learning all of this, even if you had to learn it the hard way," Ms. Perdomo said, unsmiling. She wore only one button today; it read DEMOCRACY! "I will let you take Mariela's place," she told Celia, "but only on the condition that before the start of the debate, you come completely clean to your classmates."

Celia sat in the chair, stunned. She couldn't imagine admitting everything she'd just said to the entire seventh grade.

As if she'd read her mind, Ms. Perdomo said, "You don't have to confess *all* of what you just told me, but you do have to be honest with everyone. I know you'll find the right way to explain this to them — you're great at communicating, and that's part of why I know you'd make a great seventh grade rep."

Celia nodded, silently agreeing to the condition. After Ms. Perdomo's compliment, she felt a little bit better, and she almost started to relax. But Ms. Perdomo had something else to add.

"One other thing," she said from the other side of the desk. "You're one of the top students in this school, and I approved your candidacy because you've never been in trouble before. But from now on, you can't ever claim to have an untarnished record with me."

It was the most serious she'd ever seen Ms. Perdomo, and she felt horrible for letting her down, but she knew things could have been much worse. Ms. Perdomo finally broke her stone face and cracked a smile. "You're ready for this debate, then?" she'd asked. And Celia had nodded and given her a nervous grin.

And now here she was, waiting to be introduced as a candidate for seventh grade rep. Mari would very likely be standing in this same spot later that afternoon for her first staged run-through. Somehow that knowledge made Celia feel better.

What *didn't* make her feel better was knowing that Laz was waiting on the other side of the stage with no clue that he was now running against her and not Mari. Ms. Perdomo thought it was unfair to spring such a surprise on him just an hour before the debate; it would make him doubt whatever preparations he had taken. Celia thought it might be worse for Laz to just see her across the stage from him at the last second, but she was in no position to argue with Ms. Perdomo about that.

Besides, she was the one with a degree in counseling.

After some introductory remarks from the principal that mostly had to do with staying in your seats and not booing or talking, Ms. Perdomo took the microphone and explained how the actual voting would work.

"The polls will open during the first lunch period and remain open until the end of the day. Every seventh grader will have the opportunity to vote for one candidate via secret ballot. This debate is your last opportunity to get your questions answered before you vote, so please take advantage of the democratic process." She cleared her throat away from the microphone, then said, "Without further ado, please welcome the first candidate, Mr. Lazaro Crespi."

Laz came out from the opposite side of the stage, his hands raised in the air, pumping up the crowd. Celia pulled her side of the curtain back very slightly and watched him take his spot behind the podium farthest from her side of the stage. All the kids cheered wildly, their screams and whistles and claps merging into one solid tube of noise that funneled its way right into Celia's chest. If she hadn't been so focused on breathing through her nose, she might have thrown up.

"Thank you, that's enough," Ms. Perdomo said, quieting the crowd. Some renegade whistles and claps lingered in the air as she began to speak again, this time to introduce Celia.

"Our next candidate isn't who you're all expecting, but I can assure you she's been part of this election from the very beginning. She has a few words to say before we officially begin."

People in the crowd began to mumble to one another. The symphony of voices asking "What? Who?" grew louder and louder. Celia felt the murmurs rattling in her bones, but then she heard it: a tremendous "SHHH!" from somewhere near the front of the crowd. She knew without seeing that it was Mari, projecting from her diaphragm the way Mrs. Wanza had taught her to. The mumbling quieted down and Ms. Perdomo continued with the intro, but Celia didn't register any of it. Mari's shush had quieted her own thinking and made it possible for her to finally get her mind into Presentation Mode — facts, ideas, platforms, slogans, all of them rising and falling in her brain, sorting themselves out in an organized way. Despite her nerves and her fears, she knew she just needed to get on that stage and start talking. She couldn't be more ready.

That was when she heard Ms. Perdomo say, ". . . to present Ms. Celia Martinez."

As she walked out onstage, Celia was shocked: After an initial pause, people were clapping and cheering. It sounded to her exactly like what they had done for Laz. The cheers lasted the whole walk from the stage wing to her podium. Celia felt a surge of confidence. She'd feared the worst, and so was thrilled to see that most people didn't care that she wasn't Mari. All she had to do now was come clean, state her case, and win some votes.

Laz, however, *did* notice that he suddenly had a new opponent. He stood on the other side of the stage, his mouth open and his eyes scrunched in confusion. As she looked back at him, she noticed something in the corner of her eye: In the front row on Laz's side of the stage was Raul, flailing his arms. He was trying to get Laz's attention, but Laz just couldn't seem to take his eyes off her. She stood up a little straighter, gave him a big grin, and shrugged, hoping that was enough of an apology for the moment. He seemed to remember then that he was onstage, because he finally closed his mouth, shook his head, and then shrugged back at her. He mouthed, "Good luck."

Celia leaned forward to speak into the microphone. "Fellow seventh graders," she began. "I know you expected to see Mariela Cruz standing here today. But the truth is . . ."

She scanned the crowd for Mari and found her in the second row. Mari stood up and waved, then whistled through her fingers, her now-tattered script tucked under her arm. "Go, Celia!" Mari screamed.

Celia beamed at her friend from the stage and felt like she could do anything now.

"The truth is I made Mari run *for* me, because I didn't think I could win. The speeches, the campaign ideas — they all really came from me. But I made Mari pretend they were hers. I thought she had a better chance of getting elected because she's popular. I got caught up in thinking about cliques and coolness and stuff that shouldn't really matter in an election. That was wrong of me. I now realize that it isn't up to me to decide if I can win — it's up to all of *you*. So here I am. Please forgive me, and thank you for the chance to prove that I'm the right person for this job."

"Celia rules!" Mari yelled from the second row.

When the people around Mari saw that she was totally supporting Celia, they started clapping, more curious about than upset by the candidate switch. Raul had stopped his flailing and was now sitting on the edge of his seat, hanging on her every word, a look of total shock but complete attention in his eyes. Yvette, from her spot in the fifth row, didn't even turn to her girls to start gossiping. They were waiting to see what Celia had to say.

"Thank you, Ms. Martinez," Ms. Perdomo said, calming the crowd once more. As Ms. Perdomo began talking from her spot onstage — she would be moderating the debate, and was filling in the student body on how to go about asking their questions — Celia looked out at her fellow seventh graders. She saw Yvette and her posse, all of them with attentive looks on their faces. Behind them were the twins. She saw Luz Rojas, sitting with her feet on the seat in front of her. She saw Sami, Mari's understudy, near the back of the auditorium, a sour look on her face. Maybe she wouldn't be getting Sami's vote now that Celia had made it possible for Mari to keep her part. But she couldn't control what Sami — or anyone else — thought. Celia could only do the best job possible and hope people still liked her ideas when they came from her, and not Mari.

"Now that we're clear on how the debate will proceed —"

Mari whistled loudly one more time, and Celia waved to her in the crowd. Even though she hadn't had a chance to apologize directly to Mari for everything she'd put her through, Celia knew things would be okay between them. Mari seemed proud of her, and Celia knew that soon the roles would be switched: She'd be in the audience, cheering on her best friend's performance. She couldn't wait to see her onstage doing what she did best, and she couldn't wait to tell Mari everything that had happened that morning. More than anything else, she couldn't wait to ask Mari to forgive her, though from the loudness of Mari's whistles, it seemed as though she'd been forgiven already.

Ms. Perdomo's eyes flashed as she turned to each candidate before bending down close to the mike. "And now," she said in a Presentation Mode of her very own, "let the debate begin!"

Chapter Twelve

For the first time ever, the mango-scented air in Ms. Perdomo's office was making Celia feel queasy. It wasn't any stronger than usual. It was just that Ms. Perdomo had called her here unexpectedly, the pass to the main office waiting in Celia's home-room teacher's hand when she walked in the classroom that day — the day the seventh grade student rep election results would be announced.

As she'd walked into the small, bright room, she'd noticed that Ms. Perdomo displayed no pins on her lapel that day, which also made Celia nervous. The room was empty except for the counselor, and Celia worried that maybe Ms. Perdomo had changed her mind, that she was, in fact, super-mad at Celia for having lied and was about to expel her from school for life. Celia would have to wander the streets (her mom would certainly kick her out of the house if she were a middle school dropout) and do science experiments on the sidewalk for passing pedestrians in the hopes of earning spare change.

Celia had just started worrying about where she would find cardboard boxes to build a house out of when Ms. Perdomo said, "We're just waiting on Lazaro to get down here."

Was Laz getting expelled, too? That didn't make any sense. If Laz was on his way to her office, then Ms. Perdomo wasn't about to yell at her — this must be about the election results, right? Celia decided to stop worrying for a little while — at least until she knew what was really going on.

Laz walked in a few seconds later, a huge grin plastered on his face as he turned and strolled through the door. When he saw Celia already sitting in one of Ms. Perdomo's two office chairs, his smile faded a little bit.

"Hi, Celia," he said, still standing. "Ms. Perdomo, you wanted to see me?"

"I wanted to see you both," she said brightly. She extended her hand out to the open chair and said, "Please, have a seat."

Celia hadn't seen Laz since the debate on

Friday. She looked for him at lunch to try to explain everything, but she hadn't spotted him or Raul in the cafeteria. She had seen Mari — she'd snuck into the dress rehearsal after school and watched from the very back seats of the auditorium as Mari delivered her lines flawlessly. She almost felt bad for Sami, who sat with her arms crossed in the front row, mouthing all of Mari's lines along with her until Mrs. Wanza caught her and told her to stop because it was distracting the actors onstage. Celia had been so proud of Mari that she thought she would burst.

She'd seen Mari over the weekend, too, when she went over to her house and formally apologized. Mari didn't even let her get out the words "I'm sorry" before she'd grabbed Celia in a hug and said, "I saw you in the back of the theater. Thank God you were there — I was so nervous." Celia had been about to thank Mari for being that same source of confidence at the debate.

"You were so awesome," Celia said of Mari's performance. "I totally believed you were that Roxane lady."

"No, you want to see really awesome? Let's talk about you at the debate. You were totally the winner."

"Shut up!" Celia said, blushing.

"No, really! You showed everybody that YOU were the one to vote for."

During the debate, Laz had come off as unprepared and not very quick under pressure. Celia, on the other hand, got all her opinions across while still managing to crack a few jokes and addressing all the different groups of students. She had a thoughtful and thorough answer to each question, getting everything out before she ran out of time, whereas Laz got cut off by the two-minute buzzer almost every time. She'd felt good about her performance, but that didn't mean she would win the election. After all, it was still a popularity contest. Laz had turned the buzzer's ding into a joke by the end, trying to get cut off on purpose for laughs. He was still very likable, and when it came down to names on a ballot, more people would probably remember Laz Crespi than Celia Martinez.

After more hugs and apologies and promises, Celia and Mari spent that afternoon hanging out, watching some new-to-them episodes of *Dog Whisperer*, and laughing about how none of those tips would ever work on Poochie. They'd even talked about Laz: Mari confessed to liking him a little, but that she didn't like him as much after seeing him in the debate. "Not the sharpest tool in the shed," she'd said, "but he's pretty to look at." They'd laughed all day, Mari's mom made croquetas for them to eat for lunch, and Celia wished Monday morning — and the inevitable election results — would never come.

Once Laz was settled in the chair, Ms. Perdomo cleared her throat and said, "I've called you both in to hear the news from me first, in case there are any tears."

Laz laughed out loud at this, but Ms. Perdomo shot him a stern look and he stopped. Celia was sure now that she had lost the election. This kind of move on Ms. Perdomo's part was clearly directed at her, not at Laz. She tried to make herself feel better by thinking back to hanging out with Mari that weekend and by remembering that they were tighter than ever for having gotten through all the election craziness together.

At least she'd gotten over her crush on Laz thanks to the campaign. She never had to think about him again, except that she'd be hearing him on the morning announcements a lot more now that he was seventh grade rep. But she'd get used to it. Another bright side: She'd gotten to meet and talk to a lot more of Coral Grove's students than ever before — like Raul. In fact, it was through Laz that she'd come to appreciate Raul and his campaigning smarts.

"As you both know," Ms. Perdomo went on, "the votes were tallied over the weekend. I have the results here."

She held up an already opened envelope.

Celia actually felt relieved that this would all be over with soon. Maybe Laz would ask for her input on things. She could still work to get her ideas heard; there was no reason this had to be the end of Celia's involvement with politics and student government. Besides, she always had science to fall back on, and that wasn't a bad place to be. Maybe now that the campaign was over, she could embrace her nerd-dom the way Mari had embraced her drama persona.

Just as Celia decided she had enough positive arguments for losing the election to keep herself from crying in front of Laz, Ms. Perdomo looked at her and said, "Congratulations, Celia."

She honestly thought her ears were stuffed with something, because Laz jumped in the air and said, "Yes!" But then he froze and stared at Ms. Perdomo with the same shock that was all over her own face.

"You mean Lazaro, right?" Celia said, believing, as Laz did, that he'd won.

Ms. Perdomo shook her head no.

Laz sat back in the chair, one hand on each of the armrests. He was clearly stunned, but was trying not to show it.

"It was a very close race," Ms. Perdomo said, "but Celia, you won. Your classmates voted you their official seventh grade representative." She could tell that Ms. Perdomo was holding back a smile to spare Laz's feelings. "It was, as I said, a very close race. Lazaro, I congratulate you on running an interesting and engaging campaign."

Celia couldn't believe what she was hearing. For the first time in Coral Grove Middle School's recent history, a certifiable nerd had just won a popularity contest. And that nerd was her! So it *was* possible! She couldn't believe she had doubted the voters — and herself — as much as she had.

"Celia, why are *you* crying?" she heard Laz say.

She reached up to her face and realized that she was, in fact, crying — she was just so shocked and happy, she was crying tears of joy. She jumped up from her chair and hugged Laz, who stood to keep Celia from falling on top of him.

"Oh my God oh my God oh my God," she heard herself saying. She felt like she was watching herself on TV. "I can't believe it. I can't believe they voted for me!"

Laz returned the hug despite looking like the air had just been sucked out of him. Now that Laz's back was to her, Ms. Perdomo gave Celia a huge, toothy grin and a double thumbs-up. But then she caught herself and slapped her own hand for revealing who she'd been rooting for all along.

"I've got to submit these results to the principal for them to be official," Ms. Perdomo said as she rose from her desk. "Once he signs off on them, we can make the announcement to the whole school. I just wanted you both to hear them first — I'll be right back!" As she left the room, she saw Ms. Perdomo doing a little celebratory dance in the hallway.

Once Celia freed Laz from her victory hug, he said softly, "I can't believe this."

"I know, it's like a miracle!" she squealed back. "This is so awesome!"

He wrinkled his eyebrows at her, the dark furry lines looking sad and defeated. She suddenly remembered what her winning meant for him.

"Oh, right. I'm sorry," she said. "I didn't mean — I wasn't trying to be a jerk."

She lowered her head and playfully slugged him in the shoulder. She felt so much more comfortable around him now that she just thought of him as a friend.

He gave her a shrug and said, "It's okay. I kind of knew the minute the debate was over that you would make a better representative than me, anyway." He was trying to stay cool, but Celia saw in the way he slumped forward a little that he really was disappointed. She smiled at the compliment. "Raul thought so, too," Laz added.

The memory of Raul flailing his arms from the audience just before the debate flashed in her head. She said gently, "I saw him in the front row trying to get your attention right before the debate started. What was all *that* about?"

"Oh. *That*," Laz said. She could tell that he was deliberating in his head whether to tell her the truth or not. He let out a long breath and sat back in the chair.

"The truth is," he finally said, "at first he wanted me to protest the debate and refuse to continue because, you know, it was supposed to be Mari up there, not you."

Celia slowly lowered herself back into her chair. "That's smart of him," she admitted. Raul's quick thinking kind of amazed her. "That's *really* smart. You totally would have had the right to do that. Why didn't you?"

"I don't know," he said. He was staring at Ms. Perdomo's empty chair. "I didn't think of it until after he told me, but even if I'd known I could do that, I guess I just wanted to debate you. In a way, I was happy it was you, 'cause you're, like, the toughest person to beat. I wanted to prove myself by facing you, I guess."

Celia was so flattered she knew she must have been blushing. Laz said, "Don't let that go to your head, now. It's not like I had a lot of time to make that choice. Besides, Raul changed his mind after he heard your apology."

That's when Celia remembered another apology she'd meant to give.

"I'm sorry you didn't know until that second," she said. "I came clean to Ms. Perdomo that morning, and there wasn't any time for me to —"

"No, I totally understand," Laz said. His eyes flickered with recognition. "I'm not saying anything, but I sort of understand what you guys were going through." A shy look came over his face, but he rushed past it. "I wasn't so into the idea myself at first, but Raul...he kind of — helped — me with my campaign. In fact, it was kind of his idea I run in the first place."

Celia froze in her seat, suddenly realizing that she and Raul, who was unfairly known in school as little more than Laz's sidekick, may have had the same idea about wanting to run, just with different results. Celia seemed to have more in common with Raul than she first thought — no wonder she'd felt close to him ever since that day on the basketball courts! She decided right then on a new plan, one that made everything up to Mariela and Laz (and maybe even Raul).

She turned to Laz, who was still contemplating the empty desk chair, and said, "How would you and Raul like to join me and Mariela for ice cream after school? My treat."

He gave her the first real smile she'd seen from him all morning. Celia imagined the same smile on Mariela's face once she heard the election results — and their after-school celebration plans.

"That would be sweet," Laz said. "I know Raul will be down, too. He thinks you're pretty amazing. Don't tell him I told you that."

Celia gasped. She felt her heart speed up and her hands tingle. She thought back to that day at the basketball courts when she'd "accidentally bonded" with Raul, of the way he'd blushed when he saw her in the main office on the day of the candidate speeches, of the way he'd stared at her from the edge of his seat during the debate. She couldn't help but smile.

"Meet me by our palm tree?" she joked, finally figuring out how to make Laz laugh without simultaneously being mean to him.

There was a knock behind them. Both of them turned to see Ms. Perdomo and the principal poke in through the door.

"No carnage?" Ms. Perdomo said. "Excellent. We're about to make the morning announcements, so Laz, if you want to hide out here, that's totally up to you."

"No thanks, Ms. Perdomo, I'm good." He turned to Celia and said, "I want to be in homeroom when we get the great news that Celia is our rep."

Celia slugged him in the shoulder again, smiling so hard her cheeks hurt. "He's done crying, anyway," she joked to Ms. Perdomo.

They all laughed as Laz slipped out of the room, waving good-bye and winking at Celia as he left.

"I'll see you over by the PA system," the principal said as he shook her hand. "I'm cutting the Proclamations down a bit today to give us time to announce your victory."

"Thank you, sir," Celia said.

"You're very welcome," he said, saluting her.

He walked away, stopping at the front desk to pick up his notes.

Ms. Perdomo bumped her hip into Celia's side, knocking her over a little. She regained her balance just as Ms. Perdomo said, "Are you ready, Ms. Representative?"

Celia looked up at her and smiled, nodding eagerly. *Ms. Representative*, she thought, *I definitely like the sound of that.*

Check Out

Ice Dreams

by Lisa Papademetriou

Another candy Apple book... just for you.

"What about this one?" My little sister, Amelia, held up a photograph of a woman with short hair puffed into spikes.

"She looks like an exotic cactus," I told her.

"Rosa! That's the *point*!" Amelia huffed and kicked her legs against her chair. Her toes barely scraped the salon's pale wood floor. "I want to make a *statement*!"

"A statement like, 'I'm wearing a colorful blowfish on my head'?" I asked her. "Is that really how you want to start school here?"

Amelia huffed again. Grumbling, she turned the page. "Ooooh!" Her eyes lit up.

Our mother appeared and frowned down at the photo Amelia was admiring. Blond hair with pink tips. "Not appropriate for fourth grade," Mom announced.

With a dramatic sigh, Amelia shut the hairstyle book and placed it back on the table, along with the other portfolios.

"You have gorgeous hair, Amelia," Mom told her. "You don't need a crazy cut or wild color."

"I'm sick of my hair!" Amelia wailed dramatically. She tossed her long, jet black locks over her shoulder and pretended to fuss with it, as if it had been causing a ruckus on her head.

"Fine, you can tell it to the stylist," Mom said.

"Ms. Hernandez?" The receptionist, Renee, smiled at my mother. "Angela is ready."

"Rosa, you're next," Mom told me as she took Amelia by the hand.

"Is there anything I can get you while you wait?" Renee asked me. "We have juice, tea, seltzer water, or hot cocoa."

"I'm fine, thanks," I told her. "I've got my glass of water."

"Just let me know if you need anything," Renee said before retreating to her desk.

I sat back in the plush leather chair and flipped through a celebrity magazine. Sometimes, the way people treated me in my mom's salons made me a little uncomfortable. It was bad enough when we lived in Miami, and she was southeast regional director for the Athena brand. But now they'd made her executive vice president and moved us to Chicago. When Amelia and I showed up for our haircuts, Mom let it drop that she was a bigwig from Corporate. Now everyone was falling all over themselves for our sake. But I didn't need cocoa and a chair massage — all I wanted was a trim. I had to start a new school the next day, and I didn't want to look raggedy.

I flipped another page, checking out the reviews of a couple of new movies, when I heard someone say, "Ex-*cuse* me? Are you *kidding*?"

I looked up and saw Renee blushing madly. "I'm sorry, there's been a mix-up, and someone is scheduled against your appointment."

A girl with gorgeous strawberry blond curls was standing in front of the reception desk, her arms folded across her chest. She looked like she was about my age. A woman with light brown hair placed a hand on the girl's shoulder. "Look, we made an appointment for my daughter, and we expect you to honor it." Her voice had an edge.

"What's the name again?" Renee asked.

"Jacqueline Darcy," the girl said.

Renee shook her head as she flipped through the calendar. "I don't see your name. . . ."

"Isn't another stylist available?" her mother demanded.

"I'm sorry, but we're all booked —"

"Is there a problem here?" my mother asked as she strode up to reception. She had on dark jeans and a T-shirt with a bright red cardigan, but somehow managed to look Very Official. Maybe it was the way she walked. "How can I help you?"

"There was a mistake in the booking, and this girl's appointment got bumped," Renee explained to my mother.

Mom didn't go ballistic. She just nodded. "Well, luckily, that problem is easily fixed. She can take Rosa's appointment."

I looked at the girl. Honestly, her hair looked great — she didn't even need a haircut. Still, I knew my mother's motto: "Even when the customer is wrong, they're right." I just sighed. "No problem."

Jacqueline smiled gratefully at me. "Thank you so much! I've got this really important presentation tomorrow, and I want to look decent."

Very important presentation? I wondered what that could possibly be, but decided not to ask. "Okay, well, good luck with that," I told her.

Renee stood up. "Well, if you'd just follow me, Jacqueline . . ."

"Everyone calls me Jacqui."

"I'll be back in an hour," Jacqui's mother said, giving her daughter a quick peck on the cheek.

"Thanks again!" Jacqui called as she followed Renee to the sinks.

I waved. Mom came over and pulled my long hair over my shoulder. "I'll give you a trim when we get home," she promised.

I gave her a dubious look. "You haven't cut hair in ten years."

Mom smiled. "Yeah, but I cut it for ten before that. I've still got the skills."

Renee bustled back. "Ms. Hernandez, I swear to you that has never happened before —"

Mom nodded. "And we don't want it to happen again."

Renee straightened up, nodding seriously. "Never."

"Happy customers are repeat customers," Mom told her.

"Absolutely."

Mom gave Renee a pat on the shoulder. "Great."

Renee stepped back behind her desk. She looked like someone who had just avoided a prison sentence.

"Omigosh, what do you guys think?" Amelia appeared, flipping her hair dramatically from side to side, like a model in a shampoo commercial.

"Did you get it cut yet?" I asked her. Seriously, I couldn't see a difference.

"Are you *kidding*?" Amelia looked shocked. "I got, like, half an inch lopped off!"

"Looks great, honey," Mom said.

"Yeah," I agreed. "Looks great." But I couldn't help smiling to myself a little. My best friend, Jessica, always used to refer to my little sister as a "Wannabe Drama Queen." It was just so Amelia to walk into a salon, threaten to get pink hair, and then get the world's most insignificant trim.

"Ooh, cool!" Amelia said as she bounced along on the bridge between the two ice-skating rinks.

"I know, *two* rinks!" I agreed warmly.

"No, I'm talking about the frozen yogurt place," Amelia explained. "Mom, can I get some?"

Mom dug through her purse and pulled out her red wallet. "Sure. Get me some, too. Anything chocolate. Rosa?"

"Vanilla and chocolate twist with chocolate sprinkles."

"I'm getting chocolate with chocolate sprinkles," Amelia announced.

We're a family of chocolate fiends — can you tell? Mom handed Amelia a twenty-dollar bill, and she scurried off to get our orders. The ice rinks were at the center of the indoor mall, on the first level. People munched and watched the skaters zip by in an endless circle while pop music played over the loudspeakers. There were two levels overhead, and the ceiling was made of glass.

Mom and I went down a short flight of stairs to the large rink's main entrance. A friendly woman with big hair and a big smile greeted us from behind a counter. "Hi! Welcome to Wilkinson Rinks! Do you need to rent some skates today?"

"Actually, I'm here to find out about skate classes," Mom said.

"For you?" the woman asked.

"For me," I piped up.

"And you are . . . ?"

"I'm Rosa Hernandez."

"I'm Opal Mission." She smiled, revealing perfectly even teeth. "Have you ever skated before, Rosa?" She pulled out a full-color brochure.

"She's won several awards," Mom announced.

"Mo-om." I rolled my eyes. "They were for the county — where we used to live. In Miami. It wasn't some huge achievement."

"Well, Miami's a big city," Ms. Mission said. "There must have been skaters."

"Yeah, but — skating isn't huge there," I told her. "At least, not at the place I went to."

"Don't listen to her," Mom cut in. "Rosa's a very gifted skater. She'll need an advanced class."

"Maybe we should start you out in Intermediate," Ms. Mission suggested. She shifted her body against the counter. She was overweight, but in a pretty way that made her soft-looking. She smiled kindly at me. "If you do well, you can move up."

"She needs an *advanced* class," Mom insisted, her dark eyes flashing.

Ms. Mission laughed. "You're a lady who knows what she wants, aren't you?" she asked.

"She sure is," I agreed.

Mom's scowl relaxed into a smile, and she even managed to chuckle at herself.

"Okay, Advanced it is," Ms. Mission said. "That class meets at 3:30."

Ms. Mission smiled as my mother handed over the check. "Great! We'll see you here tomorrow afternoon."

Accidentally
Fabulous

Accidentally
Famous

Accidentally
Fooled

Accidentally
Friends

How to Be a Girly Girl in
Just Ten Days

Miss Popularity

Miss Popularity
Goes Camping

Making Waves

Juicy Gossip

Life, Starring Me!

Callie for President

Totally Crushed

Wish You Were Here,
Liza

See You Soon,
Samantha

Miss You, Mina

Winner Takes All

POISON APPLE BOOKS

The Dead End

This Totally Bites!

Miss Fortune

Now You See Me...

THRILLING. BONE-CHILLING.
THESE BOOKS HAVE BITE!